WHAT BLOGGERS ARE SAYING ABOUT

A HISTORICAL NOVEL BY

AMY CECIL

I have to say that Amy Cecil is magnificent. As you read this story The Ripper comes alive in all his cunning glory. There was never a dull moment in this book as my mind was constantly on the go trying to stay one step ahead.

Alison Pridie, Alison's Blog

Cecil has done a wonderful job blending fact, romance, and suspense that has you swooning in one chapter and on the edge of your seat the next. The scenes between these two are incredible and the worry you have for Marie because the killer is out there has you biting your nails. Very well done!

Rae's Reading Lounge

Love this book. Five Stars! I couldn't put it down. I would so reread this book because it is so good. I highly recommend it.

Alexis Long, From the Heart of a Bibliophile Lair

I was BLOWN AWAY by Amy Cecil's interpretation of the infamous Jack the Ripper mystery! Amy Cecil has given her readers a twist on history that is unique and intriguing! There was drama, passion, mystery and suspense packed into the pages of this book! I HIGHLY recommend this book! Extremely well done!

Ebony Simone McMillan, This Mommy Loves to Read Blog

We all know the story of Jack the Ripper, but what you don't know is Amy Cecil's version. Perfection is the best description of Ripper that I can think of, just perfection!

Alicia Freeman, Alicia Reads Blog

Ripper is hands down one of the best erotic thrillers I have read! Amy's takes her knowledge of how to write a historical drama and dives into the erotic thriller genre. Once again, giving us another show-stopping book!

Monica Diane, BAMM PR & Blog

Ripper

A Historical Novel By
Amy Cecil

RIPPER

Copyright © 2018 Amy Cecil

All Rights Reserved in accordance with the U.S. Copyright Act of 1976. The scanning, uploading, and electronic sharing of any part of this book without the permission of the author constitutes unlawful piracy and theft of the author's intellectual property. If you would like to use materials from this book (other than for review purposes), prior written permission must be obtained by contacting the author.

FBI Anti-Piracy Warning: The unauthorized reproduction or distribution of a copyrighted work is illegal. Criminal copyright infringement, including infringement without monetary gain, is investigated by the FBI and is punishable by up to five years in federal prison along with a fine of $250,000.

This is a work of fiction. Names, characters, businesses, places, events and incidents are either the products of the author's imagination or used in a fictitious manner. Any resemblance to actual persons living or dead, or actual events is purely coincidental or used in a fictitious manner. The author acknowledges all song titles, film titles, film characters and novels mentioned in this book are the property of and belong to their respective owners.

Any views expressed in this book are fictitious and not necessarily the views of the author.

Thank you for your support of the author's rights.

Book cover design by Rebecca Weeks of Dark Wish Designs

Layout by Ellie Bockert Augsburger of Creative Digital Studios. www.CreativeDigitalStudios.com

Editing Services provided by Carl Augsburger of Creative Digital Studios. www.CreativeDigitalStudios.com

ISBN-13: 978-1725612495 ISBN-10: 1725612496

DEDICATION

*This book is dedicated to
The women whose lives were lost to Jack the Ripper.
And to the armchair sleuths who entertain us
with their wild theories and many diverse suspects.*

FOREWORD

*Entwining love, lust, judgement, murder, and mystery,
Ripper is hauntingly breathtaking.*

While we all know the murders of Jack the Ripper on paper, Amy Cecil brings him to life in Ripper. In keeping with the historical accuracy, we get a peek inside the man behind the murders and the mystery behind the women.

Combining romance, mystery, murder, and an ending that will have you holding your breath, Riper is a book that should be at the top of any readers list.

International Best Selling Author
R. L. Weeks

PROLOGUE

Known Facts About Jack the Ripper

There were 5 murders that occurred between August 31 and November 9, 1888, in Whitechapel, the East End of London that are credited to Jack the Ripper.

The canonical five victims are as follows: Mary Ann Nichols, Annie Chapman, Elizabeth Stride, Catherine Eddowes, and Mary Jane Kelly. All the victims were prostitutes.

The mutilations to the victims became increasingly severe as the series of murders proceeded.

Nichols' body was discovered at about 3:40 a.m. on Friday, August 31, 1888 in Buck's Row (now Durward Street), Whitechapel. Her throat was slit from ear to ear, but she was not missing any organs.

Chapman's body was discovered at about 6 a.m. on Saturday, September 8, 1888 near a doorway in the back yard of 29 Hanbury Street, Spitalfields. Chapman's uterus was taken.

Stride and Eddowes were both killed in the early morning of Sunday, September 30, 1888. These murders occurred within a few minutes walking distance of each other.

Stride's body was discovered at about 1 a.m. in Dutfield's Yard, off Berner Street. She received the least amount of mutilation; just having her throat cut. Many believe that this is because the murder was interrupted.

Eddowes' body was found in Mitre Square in the city of London, three-quarters of an hour after Stride's. Eddowes had her uterus and a kidney removed and her face mutilated.

Kelly's mutilated and disemboweled body was discovered lying on the bed in the single room where she lived at 13 Miller's Court, off Dorset Street. Kelly's body was eviscerated and her face hacked away. Though her organs were removed, only her heart was missing from the crime scene.

Several letters were sent to the police and the press, their authors claiming to be the killer. One letter in particular, known as the Dear Boss letter, is how the murderer got the name Jack the Ripper. There is much speculation about the validity of the letters and many believe them to be a hoax formulated by the press to sell newspapers.

Scotland Yard and the Whitechapel police interviewed several suspects from all walks of life, from butchers and doctors to London's elite society, even including the Prince of England. All interviews were futile because there was never enough evidence to charge any of them.

Jack the Ripper is one of the first murderers to earn the title of "serial killer."

The Jack the Ripper murders still remain unsolved today.

CHAPTER ONE

August 31, 1888
Whitechapel District
London, England

The early hours of the morning bring a coolness to the air that I did not expect and have not dressed appropriately for. It feels like rain. I look up to the sky and see a minimal amount of cloud cover, but that's nothing unusual. Wrapping my shawl around me in an attempt to chase the chill from my body, I shudder at the stillness of the night. I walk briskly down Commercial Road toward home.

I don't have the luxury of having a profession that would allow me to be home at this time of the morning. I am what you would consider a lady of the night. It is not something I am proud of, but selling my body pays the rent and puts food on my table. It's not uncommon for women who share the same circumstances as I do to resort to such means.

Tonight's gentleman (and I use the term loosely) wanted a little extra attention. When I explained to him that he got what he paid for, he offered to pay more. When you're like me and you need every bit of income to provide a roof over your head, you do what you have to and take the money. I couldn't refuse, and so I stayed longer than I should have. I try to convince myself that Joe won't be angry with me for being out so late and that the extra money in my pocket will abate his imminent anger, but I know better. He will be angry and it will be up to me to calm him before I become the object of his wrath.

I am so late, I think to myself as I hurry down the street. There will be no avoiding Joe's anger.

Joe and I met a little over a year ago. I remember it was Good Friday of last year. We met, had a drink together, and then agreed to meet again the next night. After our second meeting, Joe professed that he had admired me for quite some time and offered to take me in. Just like that. It was hard to believe that he wanted to move on with our relationship so quickly and when I asked him about it he said he wanted to take care of me. He knew it was too soon for us to be in love, but he hoped that if we were sharing a room our feelings would change. He wanted more from me than I wanted to give, but it was an opportunity to ensure that I had a place to sleep when I was done working. I still had to work to help with the rent, but there was a lot less pressure sharing that burden with Joe. Some would call me a user. I call myself an opportunist.

I care for Joe, I really do, but I am not in love with him, nor will I ever be. Maybe I *am* a user, because I am definitely using him. Sometimes I feel that he is more of a father figure to me than a partner. But I do what I can to keep him happy and content, which includes having sex with him occasionally. It doesn't happen very often, because he has a difficult time knowing that I have been with so many other men. But he stays and he has always helped me financially, and for that I am grateful to him. Because of all that, I know that I owe him some respect. He has been out of work the past several weeks and I have been carrying the burden, but I do it because of the times he carried the burden for me.

I should have stayed in Ireland. I should have never defied my parents to avoid a marriage that I did not want. I had family there and money was never an issue. My father was a gentleman and a landowner. I had everything that I could have ever wanted, but I was headstrong and stubborn. I was the victim of an arranged marriage that I had no intention of going through with. At the age of sixteen, I fell in love with Collier. Looking back now, I am not sure if you could call it mature love, but it was enough for me to leave the comforts that had been afforded to me my entire life. I ran off with him and married him without my father's blessing. He was of a lower class than we were and my parents thought he was definitely not suitable for the daughter of such a prestigious family. Needless to say, I was disowned and my family severed all ties with my husband and me. Not wanting to cope with the aftermath of that in Ireland, after we were married we moved to England.

At the time I didn't care about my family and was ready to have my happily ever after with the man I loved. And for a short time, we were really happy. We struggled financially, but we had each other and he made me happy. But you know what they say about counting your chickens before they are hatched. My marriage was cut short after only three years when he died in a mine explosion. After he was laid to rest, there wasn't any money to pay my passage home—not that my family would have taken me back anyway. I was just about broke and went without food for days at a time. I knew I had to do something, and so, after much deliberation, I realized that the only way I could earn an income and maintain a roof over my head was to turn tricks.

After spending some time in Cardiff, I eventually made my way to London as I heard that the Whitechapel district had many opportunities for a woman in my situation. There, I found an upscale brothel in the East End that suited me: Madame Grace's House of Pleasure. I have been in London now for four years. I have come to call this city home and I really do not see myself relocating again.

The blaring sound of a police whistle jars me from my thoughts. It's so close, perhaps only a block or two away from where I am now. *Something has happened,* I think to myself. The urgency of the whistle tells me that it is something ghastly. A murder, perhaps.

A morbid sense of curiosity overtakes my thoughts. *I have to know what has happened.* It doesn't matter that I am late and Joe is going to be so angry; my curiosity gets the best of me and I turn down the alley toward the whistle. I know exactly where this alley will take me and I begin to follow it toward Buck's Row. All thoughts of Joe being angry flee right out of my head. I have to know what the police have found. I have to know who has been killed. I have to see it for myself.

As I continue to walk down the alley toward the sound, I suddenly get the feeling that I am being followed. Breathing as quietly as I can, I listen for footsteps, but I hear nothing. Unfortunately, the lack of footsteps behind me does not keep the skin on the back of my neck from prickling. The chill in the air cuts through me like a knife and suddenly I begin to panic. My heart drops into the pit of my stomach; I know that someone is behind me and they are getting closer. I quickly turn to face whoever is there and to my surprise I see nothing. Nobody is following me. Nobody is there. I stand there for a moment, shaking my head at my ridiculousness, and then I breathe a sigh of relief. I am just being a silly fool. My mind is playing tricks on me, which is to be expected when one is walking down a dark alley in the wee hours of the morning and a possible murder has taken place only a couple of blocks away.

Turning back to continue my journey, I don't even take two steps before I ram into something hard and solid. Startled by the barrier, I reach my arms up to steady myself. I realize that I have run into a man. My gaze travels up his broad, solid chest, then to his strong arms and neck, until I finally reach his face. His eyes smolder into my skin and I find that I am unable to move. I am totally captivated by his gaze. My hand still rests on his chest, and the heat from his body is causing a burning sensation in my hand, but I cannot move it. The sensation consumes me and I find it difficult to do anything, let alone speak.

"Forgive me," I whisper meekly, as if the sound of my voice will startle him.

"Please, madam, I was the one not looking where I was going. My apologies," he says, his voice thick and sultry. The mere sound of his voice turns my legs to jelly. He speaks eloquently; I get the feeling that this man does not live in Whitechapel. *So what brings him to the East End?* I falter in my stance and he quickly reaches to catch me before I fall. When he does, I feel the glow from the gas lamp on the street cross over my face, casting a warm glow over my complexion.

"I am a fortunate man to run into someone so lovely." He brings my right hand to his lips and gives a small kiss to the back. Glorious tingles immediately run up my arm and spread over my entire body. *How can one man, one delicious man, have such an effect on me?*

Once I am able to find some semblance of normality and I am feeling a bit more composed, I notice that he is breathing heavily. "Sir, are you unwell?" I ask.

"No. My apologies, I am just in a hurry," he replies.

"Oh, then do not allow me to detain you," I say.

He gives me a slight bow and says, "Forgive me, but I must go. But I assure you, madam, we will meet again." As he rushes off, his dark cloak billows behind him. I also notice that he is carrying a bag that resembles a medical bag. *A doctor, perhaps? Maybe he is rushing to get to the hospital.*

The St. Mary's church bells chime four. *Oh, bloody hell, it is four in the morning. I must get home.* Aborting all thoughts of heading toward Buck's Row to find out what has happened, I turn back toward my original route. The morbid curiosity that led me astray has quickly vanished and I know I must hurry home. I need to go home, if not for anything but to keep the peace.

The commotion from Buck's Row slowly fades in the distance as I get closer to home.

Finally I make it to my flat. It's not a big place; in fact, some people may not even really consider it a flat, since that suggests that I have more than one room. But I like to refer to it as a flat regardless. It makes it feel bigger and better than what it actually is: one room about twelve foot square, poorly furnished with an old bedstead, two old tables, and a chair. There is no bath area in the flat; we must use the public privies down the hall. It is not the living arrangement I had hoped that I would have someday, but it is a roof over my head and place to sleep that is warm and dry. Well, dry if you avoid the leak in the ceiling every time it rains and warm if you cover up the hole in the broken window. But for now, it is home.

I open the door slowly and spot Joe sitting in the chair, waiting. I can tell by the expression on his face that this is going to be a confrontation. I expected it, but that doesn't make it any less unpleasant. But it's one that I must face if I am ever going to get any sleep tonight. I think back to the mysterious man that I ran into in the alleyway. I wonder, *What is his name? Will I ever see him again? He was so sure that we would meet again. I would like that. But where? How?*

"Where in God's name have you been, woman?" Joe shouts as I walk into the flat.

"Working."

"Until 4 am?" he barks incredulously.

"Tonight's punter wanted a little extra attention. He paid me 8d, Joe. That is double my normal rate. I could not say no. Rent is due tomorrow and, well, you've not been working. I have to do what I can."

"You don't always have to remind me, Marie!" he bellows and I can hear the anger in his voice. "You know I fucking hate that you have to sell yourself so that we can keep a roof over our heads. It makes my skin crawl to know that other men are touching you."

His anger is scaring me and I quickly become worried as to what he will do next. I know that he feels bad and I know that he is jealous; he has always provided for me in the past and it kills him that he can't now. He is just down on his luck, and I pray that things will change for us.

Trying to abate his anger, I walk over to him and give him a hug but he quickly pushes me away.

"Do you really think I want you to touch me after you have been with your punter? I cringe to think what extra attention you provided him." He pauses and then adds, "And do not fucking tell me!" Getting up from the chair, he heads for the door and storms out.

Well, I guess that is the end of that conversation. I think back to my mystery man, the cloaked man with the doctor bag. *I wonder what life would be like if he was the man in the bathroom readying himself for my bed? Would he lay with me if he knew where I had been?*

I sit down in the chair. I am too wired to sleep now. I think back to the commotion in Buck's Row. *Was it a murder? If it was, who was murdered? Perhaps it was someone I knew?*

I pull out the flask in my bag and take a swig as I contemplate the events of the last few hours. Eventually sleep overtakes my body and I fall asleep in the chair.

I really don't know how much time had passed when I am awoken by Joe yelling, "You see? Right here, this is why I don't want you walking the Whitechapel streets at night! Look, right here in the *Gazette!*" He shoves the paper in my face and I stare down at the headlines.

Horrible Murder in East London
Whitechapel Mystery[i]

I begin to read, knowing that this is the murder I had suspected last night when I heard the constable's whistle. As I read deeper into the article, I learn that the victim was a woman, thirty-five to forty years of age. Her throat was slit ear to ear, and the wound was at least an inch wide. The lower part of her abdomen was ripped open and her bowels had been pulled out and were protruding from her body. *Oh good Lord! This is horrific!*

I look up to Joe, tears welling up in my eyes. "Do you know who the woman is?" I ask him.

Shaking his head contemptuously, he replies, "No. I don't think she has been identified yet."

"It says that they have no evidence to trace the perpetrator?"

"No, which means whoever did this is still out there."

"Do you think there is any connection between this murder and the murder of Martha Tabram a few weeks ago? And then back in April, there was the murder of Emma Smith?"

He shakes his head. "I don't know," he replies gruffly.

The news in the paper today saddens me. I get up from the table and proceed out the door to the loo. After I relieve my bladder, I splash water on my face and crawl into bed. My body needs the sleep. Although Joe will fight me to the end, I still have to work tonight.

Tonight, I watched her in the alleyway.

She puts on such an act.

Was she flirting? I believe she was.

Chapter Two

September 1, 1888

I can't get the murder from the previous day out of my head. As I ready myself for work, thoughts of Mary Ann Nichols consume me. Her name was released earlier today. The way that her body was mutilated mortifies me and makes me sick to my stomach. It's brutal and ghastly and I can't think of anything else. Hopefully work will distract me.

As I grab my bag and walk toward the door, Joe asks, "Where are you going?"

I turn and give him a look that says, *Are you really asking that question?* "You know exactly where I am going. I have to work, Joe."

"Oh, hell no. You are staying put tonight," he demands.

I walk over to him and gently caress his face. Looking at him lovingly, I say, "Joe, I know you worry about me and that you make these demands for my own safety. But you know as well as I do that I have to work. I do not have a choice."

"But …"

I stop him before he continues. "I know. I will be careful." I turn and walk back toward the door. When I reach the door I hesitate for a moment, turn back, and smile at Joe. I whisper, "I'm sorry."

"I love you, Marie," he replies as I walk out the door. I wish I could tell him that I love him. I care for him deeply, but the love is not there.

Leaving my flat, I hurriedly walk down Commercial Street toward Madame Grace's establishment, which resides above the Ten Bells Pub on the corner of Fournier and Commercial streets, across from the Spitalfields Market. I pray that she has work for me this evening and that my little disagreement with Joe hasn't delayed me.

Tricks are given out on a first-come, first-served basis, so it is in all the girls' best interests to get to Madame Grace's early—even if that means you have to sit around and wait until your scheduled appointment time. Of course, the pub downstairs is always a good place to pass the time. Once evening falls, the girls that didn't get assigned appointments hang around the pub and Madame Grace's for stragglers looking for a good time. Most times, we get lucky and find a lonely man looking for comfort, but other times we just drink too much and end up stumbling home.

After arriving at the Ten Bells, I rush upstairs. When I get to the top I see my friend, Liz—or, as most folks in Whitechapel know her, "Long Liz."

"All the tricks are out, Marie," Liz states as she begins to head downstairs. "Care to join me for some much-needed libations?"

"Damn, I was hoping that I'd gotten here on time," I say.

"Don't sweat it, doll. There's always tomorrow and more men than we could bed in a lifetime." She pauses and then adds, "Besides, you might just meet the man of your dreams downstairs." I scoff at her, turn around, and proceed down the stairs to the pub. I might as well make the best of things. A drink sounds really good.

Liz and I sit down at the bar. "What'll yawl have?" Domenic, the bartender asks.

"Whiskey, straight up," Liz replies.

He looks at me. "I'll have the same," I reply.

"Quiet night tonight, ladies. Not sure you will find much here," Dom states.

Liz gives Dom an annoyed look and then turns to me. "Come on, Marie. Let's find someplace to sit. We can stay here for our one drink and then maybe we might have better luck at the Queen's Head or the Princess Alice."

Liz and I sit at a table quietly drinking our drinks. My mind wanders to thoughts of my mystery man from the alleyway last night and I wonder if I'll ever see him again. I begin to envision us having a passionate love affair, and that the handsome man takes me away from the hellhole that has become my life. Lost in thought, I am roused when Liz prods, "What gives, Marie? You look like you have a story to tell." I blush at her words and at the fact that I have been caught daydreaming. "Don't go all quiet on me now. You must tell me what web you are spinning in that pretty little head of yours!"

I shake my head at her enthusiasm. She is going to be thoroughly disappointed when she learns that there is not much to tell.

"It's really nothing, Liz, honest," I reply.

"It is something. I can see it in your eyes. You have that far-off look in your eyes, as if you were dreaming about a tall, dark, and handsome stranger. I must know. Therefore, you must tell me."

I laugh. She doesn't realize how close to the truth she is. I *was* dreaming about a tall, dark, and handsome stranger. "I just met someone last night and I can't seem to get him out of my head," I say.

"Who? What is his name?" she asks.

I chuckle and say, "I don't know." Hearing the words aloud makes me realize what a fool I am. Of course I don't know his name and I know that a man like that, a gentleman, would not frequent the East End. *So then why was he there?*

"What? What do you mean you don't know?" she admonishes.

"I ran into him in the alley last night, right as the police whistles were alerting everyone of the murder in Buck's Row. We exchanged a few words, but never our names. He was indeed tall, dark, and handsome, and I believe he was a doctor—at least, he was carrying some sort of medical bag. He was in a hurry and we didn't have time to talk. Perhaps if he is a doctor, he was rushing to the hospital or something. That's all I know."

"I can't believe you didn't get his name. Have I not taught you anything, you silly girl?" Liz had a way of always making you feel like you were not as smart as she. I don't believe she did it maliciously, but she did it all the same.

"I guess I am a poor learner," I reply. I'm not in the mood to get into an argument with her; I've had enough of those at home these days. Thankfully, Liz drops the subject and we continue to enjoy our drinks.

The silence between us continues to lengthen and eventually I feel that something needs to be said to break the tension. "I guess we shall be walking the streets tonight." I look around the pub. "I believe Domenic is right, it's not looking very promising here." As I continue to look around the pub, hoping to find a client to occupy my evening, I take notice of a cloaked man standing just inside the doorway. *Bloody hell! It can't be!* I close my eyes and rub them. They are playing tricks on me. I open them again and the cloaked man is still there. *Bloody hell! He's here!*

I stare at him relentlessly, willing him to turn and look at me. I have to be sure that it's the man I encountered last night. Finally, he turns toward me. Spotting me, his eyes lock with mine and I see a look of recognition come across his face. He begins to head my way. *No! I'm not prepared to see him again.* I reach up to my hair to make sure that it is still in place. Looking down at my dress, I realize I should have chosen something better. *Why did I not choose a better dress?* I ask myself and then provide myself with the answer. *Because you don't have one, Marie. You're a mess.*

Grasping hold of her arm, I say in almost a whisper, "Liz! He's here!"

"Who?" she asks.

"The man from last night."

Her eyes follow mine and we watch the man approach our table. As he steps up to greet us, I can feel the wetness on my hands as they begin to perspire. "It's you," he says with surprise, looking directly at me.

"And it's you," I reply.

"I wasn't sure I would ever see you again," he states. Liz, who is totally consumed by his presence, is also looking quite shocked by the fact that this beautiful man knows me. I don't think she believed my story, but now here he is in the flesh.

I smile graciously at him and then reply, "We never exchanged names. My name is Marie."

"It is an honor to meet you, Marie. I am Jackson Kent, but my friends call me Jax. I hope that you will do the same," he says as he takes my hand and kisses the back of it, lingering with his lips pressed against my skin. When he releases my hand, he looks over at Liz and says, "And your friend?"

"Elizabeth Stride, sir," Liz says as she extends her hand to him. He bends down and kisses her hand as well, but does not linger like he did with me. "A pleasure to meet you, madame."

"A pleasure," Liz replies.

"I hope I am not interrupting anything," he says, his eyes never leaving my own. This man who now I can clearly see in the candlelight of the pub mesmerizes me. He is just as beautiful as I thought him to be. And those eyes! He has striking grayish-blue eyes that I swear can see right through me, all the way down to my knickers.

"Of course not," I reply. "Please, if you can, join us," I add.

"I thought you would never ask," he says as he pulls up a chair and sits at the table.

"Forgive me, I think I see someone over there that I know. Will you excuse me?" Liz says as she gets up from the table. She turns away from Jax and winks at me, then walks over to the bar where I see her begin to converse with Dom.

"So, Marie, what brings you to a place like this?" Jax asks.

"Really? You can't be serious, asking someone like me a question like that," I reply. Surely he is jesting with me.

"Someone like you?" he asks. "And what, pray tell, would you describe as someone like you?"

"Seriously?" When he doesn't respond to my question, I add, "Well, if you must know, I'm looking for work," I reply. I could lie to him, but really, what purpose would that serve? He should know up front what I do and what I am. I will not get involved in something that is based on half-truths and lies. I see enough of that every day in my line of work. I can tell that Jax is different. The fact that he is here makes me want to start this the right way, if we are starting anything at all.

"I see," he says and then adds, "So, is it fair to assume that you are looking for a client this evening?"

I smile at him. "Yes, it is definitely fair to assume such a thing."

"And if I wanted to be that client? Would you?" he asks.

"Jax, I ..."

Before I can finish what I was about to say, he takes my hand and says, "Look at me." His words are so commanding that everything in me wants nothing but to obey him. My eyes go directly to his and I am lost. "I have thought about you every minute since we encountered each other in the alleyway last evening. Tell me that you have not thought about me. Tell me that you don't feel this incredible connection between us," he demands. I have no words as I continue to stare at him. "Tell me, Marie!"

Breathlessly, I reply, "Jax ... yes, I have thought about you."

"Then it is settled. I shall be your client this evening," he replies.

I smile at him and he adds, "What are you drinking? Whiskey?"

"Yes," I reply, "straight up."

"Good. I shall be right back." As he walks over to the bar, I think to myself, *How did this evening change so quickly?* First I was worried about making any sort of money tonight, and now I'll be spending the night with him. I must be dreaming. Pretty soon I shall hear Joe bellowing something that shall awake me from my dream-filled slumber. I just know it. But as minutes pass and I hear nothing except the noise in the pub, I know without a doubt that I am not dreaming.

Jax returns with two drinks in hand. He sits one down next to my half-finished one and drinks his in one swallow. He says, "So, Marie, what shall we do this evening?" I can't help but laugh at his words.

"I think we both know what we'll be doing this evening, or at least how this evening will end, don't you think?"

"You may be pleasantly surprised, Marie. I think the outcome of our time together tonight will definitely not be something you expect."

Feeling a little unsettled by his words, I say, "Well then, perhaps you should enlighten me. Don't you think I should know up front what you plan to do with me?"

He laughs. "And ruin the surprise?"

"I don't like surprises," I say petulantly.

He laughs again. "I understand you are being cautious, Marie, but I can assure you that I won't hurt you and I will pay you well for your services. But I will not give away the surprise. So don't ask me again."

There is an awkward silence between us that I feel compelled to break. I brush off my fear and say lightly, "Well then, I guess I shall be surprised." I pause for a moment and then add, "I believe the important question is where we shall go."

He leans over and whispers in my ear, his hot breath causing the skin on my neck to prickle. "That, my dear lady, is already taken care of. You shall come to my home. I have a beautiful home in the West End that I am sure you will love," he says in a deep, sultry voice that causes my legs to turn to rubber and the wetness to pool between my thighs. It is a good thing I am sitting.

Suddenly a bit unsure of this situation, I ask, "Where do you live?"

"St. James Park," he replies casually, as if that name means nothing.

"Go on! Really?" I reply.

"Yes, I have a home at St. James Park."

"I see! That is quite a distance." I am a bit unsure about going so far away from home with him, especially with a ghastly murderer on the loose. I take a long look into his eyes and I see only kindness and strength within him.

"I have a carriage. It should take less than an hour."

I am torn. I know that being away from home at such a distance could cause all kinds of calamities if I'm not careful. I do not know this man, but something inside of me tells me I can trust him. Still, perhaps that is just because every fiber of my being wants to be with him. And then there is Joe. I cannot be late another night without causing another argument, and travelling that distance means I would definitely not get home at what Joe would call a decent hour. I look over at Jax and I see the desire in his eyes. *Can I really pass up this opportunity because I need to be cautious? Hell no! I am not a cautious woman and I will bloody do what I damn well please.*

"Well, what are we waiting for then?" I say and proceed to down my second drink. He laughs and holds out his hand as he helps me up from the table. He leads me out of the pub and to his carriage as if I am a princess.

Does she know that I'm always with her?

Chapter Three

We ride through the streets of London heading west on our way to Jax's home. I have been outside of Whitechapel only a few times the whole time that I have lived here, but it has never been as exciting as this. I look over at the handsome man sitting next to me and I still cannot believe that I am here, with him. "May I ask you something?"

"Of course," he replies. "You may ask me anything."

"I assume that a man like you does not normally frequent the East End. But I have seen you twice in Whitechapel. What brings you there?"

"Let us just say that I have business in Whitechapel," he replies. Pausing briefly, he then says, "Did I tell you that you look lovely tonight?" I smile at him. "So, Marie, tell me, what is the rate for a woman like you?" I take notice that he swiftly changes the subject as if he doesn't want me to know his business in Whitechapel.

Assuming that this man has more money than all my past customers combined, I realize that I can probably make a small fortune tonight. But then again, I don't want to scare him off or lie to him by suggesting more than I am worth. I look at him curiously, trying to gauge his interest in me. He appears quite interested, but I learned a long time ago that appearances can be deceiving. So I decide to err on the side of caution and give him the truth. "4d, sir," I reply humbly.

"4d!" he exclaims. "Why, that is an outrage! A beautiful woman like you should take nothing less than double that."

"Forgive me, sir, but Whitechapel is not the most lucrative district. The majority of its inhabitants are quite poverty stricken. I think I would be laughed at if I suggested more."

"Nonsense! Tonight, my dear, you are under my care and I can assure you that you will be paid much more than 4d for your time," he states. I find myself curious as to what he means by *under his care*.

When we turn down toward the park, I notice that the city is alive despite the late hour. Excitement is pulsing through my body and I begin to get anxious as we approach his home. The carriage begins to slow as we pull up to a beautiful home that abuts the park. The driver disembarks from his post and walks over to the door to open the carriage. Jax steps out first and turns, reaching his hand inside for mine. Taking his hand, I begin to emerge from the carriage. Never in my life have I felt like such a lady. A girl could get used to this.

He leads me up the steps and swiftly opens the door, gesturing for me to walk through in front of him. He follows behind and as I stand in the entryway in utter awe of what I see, an older gentlemen approaches. He says, "Good evening, sir."

"Good evening, Rothschild." Jax reaches over and gently lays his hands on my shoulder. He sends chills down my body as he leans in close to my ear and says, "May I take your wrap?" I nod and release my hold on my shawl, which delicately falls into Jax's hands. "Rothschild, we shall be in my study. Will you take care of this?" he says, handing my wrap to Rothschild.

"Of course, sir," he replies and then adds, "Shall I have a tray prepared?"

"Yes, that would do nicely. Keep it simple, Rothschild. I know how you tend to go overboard," he admonishes slightly. He then adds, "And the Chateau Haut-Brion Bordeaux, if you will?"

"Yes, sir."

Jax takes my hand and leads me through the foyer to a room off to the right. My guess is that this is his study. We walk past the elegant staircase, which climbs up one side of the wall and then crosses overhead. The dark wood banister is the star attribute of the staircase, accenting it all the way to the top. This entryway is stunning, masculine, and very beautiful. I can only imagine what the rest of the house looks like, and my thoughts wander to the bedrooms upstairs. Then a horrid thought occurs to me. *I hope he is not expecting me to stay the night. Oh goodness, I cannot allow that to happen. Joe would be furious.*

We enter a room that is just as beautiful as the entryway. It too is accented in dark woods, with emerald-green curtains and dark upholstery on the furniture. "This is my study. I spend most of my time here and so it is always my room of choice. There are many rooms in this house, but I only seem to frequent a couple of them. I'm saddened to say that most of the house goes uninhabited."

"It's lovely," I say to him. *Yes, a girl could definitely get used to this.*

He does not say anything further, but just stares at me. After several minutes, I begin to feel self-conscience and start to fidget.

"Are you uncomfortable?" he asks as he moves in closer.

"Uh, no."

He steps closer. "But you are fidgeting?" He is now standing right in front of me, close enough to feel his warm breath on my neck.

"You were staring," I reply in a whisper.

"I was. Do you know why?" he asks, keeping his face close to my right ear. My skin is prickling all over and I feel as if I am about to faint.

"No," I say weakly.

"I was staring at your beauty. This home, these surroundings, they suit you. You are not meant to be walking the streets of Whitechapel."

I have to laugh at his idealism. "I may not be meant for walking those streets, Jax, but in the real world, I have no other choice."

Jax takes a couple of steps away from me as Rothschild walks in with a serving cart. On it is a tray of watercress and pâté. Next to the tray are a bottle of wine and two wine glasses. Jax walks over to the cart as Rothschild takes the wine and begins to pour us each a glass. "Thank you, Rothschild, that will be all." Rothschild nods and then turns to leave us. "Rothschild, be sure to inform Carlton that there is a possibility that I will be needing the carriage later," Jax calls after him.

"Of course, sir," he replies and exits the room.

"Now where were we?" he asks as he moves in close again.

I smile and say, "May I ask you a question?"

"Of course. I have already told you that you can ask me anything," he replies.

"Are you expecting me to sleep here?"

He chuckles. "Ah, the question of the night," he says but does not elaborate.

The silence is killing me and it only makes me more curious to know what his plans are. I begin to get nervous and question my judgment in coming here.

Finally he says, "You asked a question, and yes, you deserve an answer. However, I would rather wait to see how the night progresses. Can I ask for your patience until we learn more about one another? I believe then all your questions will be answered."

I doubt that very much. As my patience dwindles, the questions just keep on coming.

"Are you hungry?" he asks. "Please ..." He gestures toward the tray.

I am not particularly hungry, but I do not want to offend my host either. I take a watercress and the smile on his faces tells me that I have pleased him. Curiously, I find that I am very happy at that prospect.

"Marie, please sit," he says as he walks over to the settee and takes a seat himself. I sit in the chair across from him, feeling uneasy and unsure again. It is as if I am riding in a train car elevated from the ground with tight turns and steep slopes. My stomach is in a flutter and my nerves are shot.

"Forget about patience. I've never been a patient man and I will answer your question." He pauses and then adds matter-of-factly, "I would like you to stay the night."

"Oh, Jax, as much as I would love to, I can't," I reply. There is no way I can spend the night here and not come home until tomorrow. Joe would never get past that. He would be worried sick and would think that I had met the same fate as Mary Nichols.

"Is there someone else?" Jax asks.

I hesitate for a moment. In my mind, there really is not. But I do owe Joe some sort of acknowledgement. "Possibly," I reply.

"Possibly?" he questions. "I am not sure I quite understand your response, Marie. Either there is another man in your life or there is not."

"There is and there isn't. I live with a man. A man who loves me very much, but also a man that I am only with due to the gratitude I owe him. I do not love him, but I do respect him. It is out of that respect for him that I cannot stay here. I promise you will get what you pay for, but you must have your driver take me back to Whitechapel before the sun comes up."

"Let's forget for a moment that you are being paid to be here and let me ask you a question. Do you want to be here, money or not?"

"I do," I reply sadly.

"And that makes you sad?" he asks.

"It does."

"And why is that?" he prods.

"I am ashamed to say it, sir." I look down at the floor because the last thing I want to do is look at him. My heart is breaking at what I am not telling him and I am praying that he does not make me say it.

He gets up from the settee and walks over the chair in which I am sitting. To my surprise, he kneels down in front of me. He places his hand under my chin and guides my face up. "Look at me, Marie." When our eyes meet, I feel the same connection I did the night I ran into him in the alley. And by the look in his eyes, I know he feels it too. "Tell me," he pleads.

I breathe in deeply and reply, "Of all the men I have encountered in my line of work, I have never wanted to be in their company, until now." I look around the room and then continue, "But we are from two different worlds. I know that after tonight, I shall never see you again. And that makes me sad."

"You give me a lot of credit. You really do not know much about me to be so trusting. I could be the recent murderer of Whitechapel for all you know."

"I know you will not hurt me," I say confidently.

"Pain is relative, Marie. Everyone experiences pain. It is the level of pain that determines what we can handle and what we cannot. When you say that I won't hurt you, it is based on your level of tolerance; the scale by which you measure pain."

He is speaking beyond my comprehension and I'm not understanding what he's trying to say. I take another sip of my wine and decide to remain quiet and anxiously wait to hear what he has to say next.

But he does not speak and we sit in silence. Not having any words to breach the silence between us, I instead admire my surroundings. For a brief moment, I envision what it would be like to be mistress of this house. Just a moment, then the realization of my life crashes down on my shoulders.

Jax breaks the silence and says, "Marie, you said that you would like to stay with me, but that you couldn't."

"I cannot stay here. I told you, I must return back to Whitechapel before sunrise." I was beginning to worry about why he would want me to stay here. Something was not right, but I could not put my finger on it.

"But you said you would like to stay here," he says.

Hesitantly, I reply, "I would. But ..."

He interrupts me before I can finish and says, "I will return you to Whitechapel before the sun rises, but before you go back, I have a proposition for you. Can you stay long enough to hear what I propose?"

I believe he senses my hesitation and apprehension about what is happening here. I reply, "I can do that. But it is getting awfully late, and if you are going to use my services tonight, we really need to get on with it."

He laughs. "I assure you, you will not leave here without your fee. You have my word on that." He continues to laugh while I wonder to myself how good his word is. I am beginning to think that he has cost me a night's wages.

"Sit, please." He gestures toward the royal blue satin-covered chair and I follow his direction and sit down. He begins to pace around me, which does not help to settle my uneasiness.

"My proposition is this," he begins. "You stated that you earned 4d per trick. Correct?"

"Yes."

"And, on a normal night, how many tricks do you do in one evening?"

I cannot help wonder where he is going with this. "Usually only one, but if it is a good night, I can get two in."

"Very well. Let us be generous and say on average you earn 8d a night. What if I told you that you could earn one crown a night and only have to be with one man? Would you like that?" he asks.

"Go on! You can't be serious. There is no man in Whitechapel that will pay a crown a night to be with me."

"Perhaps not, but I don't reside in Whitechapel," he replies.

"You?"

"Yes, me. It could be yours as long as you understand that I expect certain things of you," he replies.

"Rules?"

"Yes, you could call them rules. But we can talk about those later. Right now, I want to know if this proposition interests you."

"So you would be the man?"

"I would," he states.

I look at him curiously and wonder how I got here. He was a handsome stranger that I ran into in an alley. I had hoped that I would see him again but never expected that I would. Now I find myself sitting in his study negotiating what appears to be a long-term arrangement. An arrangement that could make me a very wealthy woman.

"And how long will this arrangement last?" I ask.

He shrugs. "I am not sure. I suppose until one of us tires of the other," he replies.

"And what if we fall in love?" I ask him.

He casually walks over to me and stands behind the chair in which I am sitting. Placing his hands on my shoulders, he bends over the chair back and whispers in my ear, "Do not misunderstand, Marie." He pauses and nuzzles his nose into my neck. "I will not fall in love. Love is not something that I ever wish to entertain." His breath is hot on my skin causing my neck and arms to prickle with pleasure. "But I will tell you this." He pauses, breathing close to my ear. "I don't make love either. Instead, I will fuck you like you have never been fucked before." He kisses the spot right behind my ear, sending shivers all through my body. My breath hitches and I realize that it is a good thing that I am sitting down. My legs do not have the strength to hold me. His left hand moves from my shoulder and slides down in front of my throat. He places it over my throat, applying light pressure, and says, "Never forget that I am paying you for your services." The sultry sound of his voice causes a pool of wetness between my legs. Never in all my days have I been so aroused. He may not fall in love with me, but I dare myself not to fall in love with him.

He steps away from the chair and walks around to face me. "Do we have an agreement?"

I do not answer him right away because my body is still trying to get over the state of arousal he just put me in. "If I may, Jax, I still have some questions."

"Then, please, ask away," he says and sits down on the chair across from me.

"Will I be allowed to go back to Whitechapel at any time?"

"Yes. I will expect you to be in the house by six o'clock in the evening until six o'clock in the morning. During the day, if you need to take care of things at home, or if you want to explore this part of London, Rothschild will be able to secure a carriage for you."

"Thank you." I pause and then add, "And what shall I tell my, er ... ugh, *friend* who lives with me?"

"The truth. I have nothing to hide from anyone." He waits to see if I respond and then adds, "I understand he has been out of work. I'm sure the crown that you will receive each day that you are here will keep him pacified."

"And what about Madame Grace?"

He quickly glances up and then looks back at me. "You do not need to worry about Madame Grace. I will ensure that she is duly compensated as well." He then continues, "Any more questions?"

I want to ask him so much more, but I get the impression that I am irritating him. He wants a yes or no from me. I want this man in my bed more than anything. I want to feel his strong arms around me as I scream his name in the night. I want him to consume me. "Yes, Jax, we have an agreement." The words come out of my mouth before I have a chance to change my mind. *Who am I kidding? I could not change my mind even if I wanted to.*

"Very well then. I am going to take you back to Whitechapel now. You will spend tomorrow getting your things in order, speaking to your friend, etc. I will pick you up at Madame Grace's tomorrow promptly at six."

All my life I had to fend for myself. I made all of the decisions that impacted my life. Yes, I had been told about appointments from Madame Grace, but that was work. Never in all my years did I have someone tell me what to do and where to be in such a way that made me want to worship at their feet. But something about this man makes me want nothing more than to drop to my knees before him.

CHAPTER FOUR

September 2, 1888

As Jax's carriage begins to slow toward my flat, he reaches over and touches my arm. "I'm very much looking forward to our arrangement, Marie."

His words make me blush as I reply, "As am I."

He moves in close and I am sure that he is going to kiss me. Bracing myself for the velvety feel of his lips against mine, I find that I am disappointed when he begins to speak. "Your fee for this evening," he says as he holds his hand out to me with the 8d clearly visible.

Taking the money from him, I thank him as I turn to get out of the carriage. He touches my arm again and I stop and turn back to face him. "Until tomorrow, my pet," he says. I nod and disembark from the carriage. Everything in me is telling me not to leave him. I do not want to leave, but yet, I know I have to.

Lingering on the walk next to the carriage, I wait until it drives off. As it disappears into the night, I look down at my clenched hand encasing the 8d Jax gave me. I am awestruck as I realize that he paid me. He paid me for absolutely nothing. *Who is this man?*

I quickly scurry toward my flat. As I walk, my thoughts retrace back through tonight's events. Jackson Kent. Even his name sounds classy. I smile as I think about his exceptionally good looks and refinement. I pinch my arm, convinced that all of this is a dream. *Is he real? What am I thinking? Have you lost your mind, Marie?* He may be interested now, but he will quickly tire of me.

He is not my Prince Charming and he is not going to sweep me off to his castle. But I can do this. For now, he wants me. So I will do this, for I know that I will feel like a queen for a few days at least.

Reality consumes me as I get closer to my home. I worry about how I am going to break this all to Joe, as I know that he will be furious when he is told that I will be gone indefinitely. At least my arrival home tonight is not as late as I was yesterday. Perhaps that will put Joe at ease a bit. *Or perhaps not.*

Walking through the door, I find that Joe is not sitting at the table waiting up for me as he usually does. I look over to the bed, empty. Joe is not here. Perhaps he is down the hall in the loo. I sit down in the chair, yesterday's papers lying on the floor at my feet. The headlines catch my eye, bold and glaring. *Who was Mary Ann Nichols and what would cause someone to murder her so brutally?* I wonder.

I push the paper aside. I can't think about this anymore. It's one murder. People are murdered every day. Unfortunately, that's just how the world is. Realizing that Joe must be out, I get up from the table and walk over to the bed. Suddenly, I am really tired. So many changes lie ahead for me tomorrow. The best way to face them is with a good night's sleep.

Crawling into bed, I lie there with dreamy thoughts of Mr. Kent. It doesn't take long for me to fall into a deep, dream-filled slumber.

I wake to hear yelling, lots of yelling. "Marie, darling! Marie, my love!" Stirring, I turn to face the door as it opens and Joe storms in. "You're home!" he yells, surprised. The way he is slurring his words and speaking rather loudly, I know that he has been drinking.

"Joe, hush up. You will wake up the entire neighborhood."

"Do not tell me what to do, woman!" he yells.

Jesus, Mary, and Joseph, what I am I to do now? I hate when he gets to drinking. He is so belligerent and at times can be quite violent. I am not in the mood for violent Joe, so in an effort to contain his temper, I rise from the bed and go over to him. "Hello, love," I say.

"Hello, Marie! I've been drinking. You should have been drinking with me."

"I know, I'm sorry I wasn't, but I'm so glad that you're home. I've been waiting for you."

He looks down at me and says, "You have?" Smiling, he adds, "Why don't you show your man how glad you are that he's home?" Suddenly thoughts of Jax enter my mind. He said that I was to be exclusive to him, that I was not to be with another man. What do I do now?

I know if I don't give Joe what he wants, I will end up battered and bruised. Although I am used to his drunken abuse, I believe it is best to give him what he wants and assure Jax that it will never happen again. Besides, our agreement has not technically begun yet, not until tonight at six.

"Come on, baby, I would love to show you." I guide him over to the bed. He stands next to the bed as I drop to my knees. Repulsed by what I am about to do, I try to imagine that I am kneeling at Jax's feet. My eyes make contact with his and I reach up to undo his belt, but his hand grabs onto my hair and tugs. He is rough, but I maintain eye contact with him to show him that he is not hurting me. If I show any sign of discomfort, he will make it worse.

"Oh baby, you always know exactly what I need," he says as he sways a little. Removing his belt and undoing his trousers, he sways again and I pause briefly. As I reach up to continue, he says, "Oh Marie, I need to sit down, love." Swaying more, he basically falls onto the bed. Still on my knees, I wait and see what he does. Luckily for me, he falls backwards and passes out.

Relief washes over me. I never minded servicing Joe before. I mean really, he has done so much for me that I always felt it was some sort of payment. But after spending the evening in Jax's company, the thought of touching any other man repulses me.

I struggle to move Joe up on the bed. At least I can get his feet from dangling off the side. Once he is in a more comfortable position, I leave him alone and allow him to sleep. We still need to talk about everything, but that conversation needs to wait until he is sober. I look out the window and see that the sun is up. Now is as good as a time as any to get my day started. I find that I have more of a spring in my step knowing that tonight I will be with Jax. For now, I don't have to worry if I will have work or whom I may end up with. Tonight, I belong to Jackson Kent.

Several hours later, Joe wakes in an irritable state. "My fucking head," he mumbles as he rubs his temple. I remain quiet, as I am not sure if he is one hundred percent sober, and I wait to see what he says next. He says, "You look beautiful this morning." I am wearing my best dress. It isn't much, but it is all I have. Jax told me not to bring anything with me, that he would provide me with whatever I need. I'm not so sure he knows what I'll need, but I trust him and prepare to bring nothing with me. "Why are you wearing your best dress?" Joe asks suspiciously.

"Joe, it's four in the afternoon. Even I would not consider this morning." I pause for a moment and then add, "You must have had a rough night. How are you feeling?"

"Don't ignore my question, Marie! Why the fuck are you all dressed up?" he demands.

"Because I want to, ok? I felt like dressing up!" I yell. "Now tell me how you feel," I demand right back at him.

"Fuck, like a horse stepped on my head." He sits down in the chair and goes back to rubbing his temples.

"I know this is not the best time, but I really need to talk to you," I say.

"Babe, you know you can talk to me anytime."

"I know, but I am afraid you are not going to like what I have to say."

He looks at me skeptically. "What the fuck, Marie? What now?" Before I can answer, he adds, "Did another fucking whore get murdered?"

"No, nobody got murdered. But what I have to say is important. Just promise that you will hear me out before you make any comments."

"Yeah, whatever," he says, annoyed.

"I've met someone," I say.

He looks at me and I can see the vein appear that protrudes across his forehead when he is angry. "Are you leaving me, Marie?" he says with a sadness in his voice that I did not expect.

"Not exactly. You see, the man I met wants to hire me exclusively. He wants to pay me a crown a day, Joe. A whole bloody crown," I say, trying my hardest to convince him that this is real, although I am still having trouble believing it myself.

"You're dreaming, girl. Nobody around here has that kind of money. And surely they would not waste it on a common whore." His words cut like a knife. *So tell me what you really think about me.*

I do my best not to let my hurt feelings show and continue, "I'm not dreaming, Joe. His name is Jackson Kent and he lives at St. James Park, in the West End."

"I know where bloody St. James Park is, Marie, you don't have to tell me," he bellows.

"Sorry," I say meekly. *Why does he insist on yelling at me all the time and treating me as if there isn't a brain in my head? It never used to bother me much, but now that I have spoken with a true gentleman, it grates on my nerves. In fact, I hate it.*

"There is more to this that you are not telling me, Marie. What the fuck is going on?" Joe is more than annoyed now; he is definitely angry.

"I have to live with him. I am free to come and go, but I am supposed to be back at his home at six each evening and remain there until six the next morning. I can return to Whitechapel during the day, but he was explicit that I would sleep there each night."

"Each night?"

"He has asked that I live with him indefinitely, basically until he tires of me. He will pay me one crown every night I sleep at his home as long as I follow his rules."

"Rules? Do you really know what in the hell you are getting yourself into? This sounds bad, Marie, real bad."

"I don't know all the rules yet; he said he would go over them tonight. He has already talked to Madame Grace. He is paying her too."

"Fuck, Marie! I forbid it. Something is not right with this and you are not going with this Mr. Kent."

"I am, Joe. I'm sorry, but you can't stop me."

"The fuck I can't!" He lunges for me and grabs me by the throat. He squeezes my throat tightly and I can barely get a breath through. After several seconds, he throws me against the wall and I fall to the floor. "Get this through your head: you are my whore. You belong to me and you are not fucking going anywhere," he says and then he storms out of the flat.

If he really thinks I am going to pass up this opportunity, well, I've got news for him.

At half past four, I step outside and walk to the spot where Jax dropped me last night. And to my surprise, a carriage is waiting. I walk up and look at the driver curiously. He turns to me and says, "Miss Marie?" I nod and he adds, "My name is Jasper. I will be your driver throughout the duration of your stay with the Master.

Master?

He works his way down from the carriage and comes around to my side. Opening the door, he says, "Allow me, miss."

As I step into the carriage I hear my name being called. "Marie! Marie, don't do this!" Joe calls after me.

I continue to step inside the carriage. Sitting down, I look out the side window back at Joe. He is running toward the carriage, but we move on and there is no chance of him catching up with us. I hate to say it, but I am relieved. I am very much looking forward to what life with *Master* Kent will be like.

Headstrong and stubborn! It's one of the things that drew me to her in the first place.

Chapter Five

September 2, 1888

When we arrive at Jax's home, Jasper helps me from the carriage and escorts me into the house. Rothschild greets me at the door and gestures for me to follow him. We are climbing the stairs and I suspect that he's taking me to my room. We pass several rooms and continue down the hall. When we reach the end of the hall, in front of us is a set of double doors. On the walls on each side of the double doors are single doors. Rothschild opens the right-hand side door and waves me inside. The room is absolutely stunning, decorated in many shades of crimson. It's breathtaking and sensual all at the same time. Satin adorns the bed covering, with sheer lace draped over the large canopy. It's a sanctuary and I absolutely love it.

"Dinner will be served promptly at seven." He walks over to a pair of interior doors and opens them, revealing a beautiful wardrobe. "Mr. Kent expects that you dress for dinner. You may choose anything you wish from here." I walk over to the open doors and am astonished by what I see inside. So many dresses, lovely dresses. Dresses that I would never be able to afford in this lifetime.

"Thank you, Rothschild. And where is dinner served?"

"In the main dining room. If you make your way downstairs at half-past six, I will make sure that you have an escort to the dining room." He pauses and then adds, "Do not be late. The Master does not like tardiness."

Rothschild leaves the room and I am left alone. I walk through the room admiring all the pretty and very elaborate furnishings. Glancing around the room, I see another door. *Where does that lead?* I wonder. I walk over to the door and turn the knob. It's locked. I make a mental note to ask Jax about it.

I walk back to the open wardrobe and look through the dresses. I am totally overwhelmed. *How do I pick just one? Did he buy all these dresses just for me? Will they fit? Surely I won't be here long enough to wear them all.*

Shuffling through them, I find a lovely gray dress. It's modest and very simple; I am hoping that its modesty will keep me from looking like the whore that I am. I sit down on the bed and take in my surroundings. I'm really here in this beautiful home and in this beautiful room. I wonder what I could have possibly done to deserve all this. I'm sure that this is a dream—to confirm my suspicions, I pinch my skin again. *Ouch!* Nope, definitely not a dream.

Suddenly, there is a knock at the door. I walk over to the door and open it. I am expecting to see Jax, but to my surprise it is a young woman dressed in a maid's uniform. She is shorter than me and has her soft brown hair pinned up in a conservative bun. Her eyes are friendly and she is smiling. "Hello miss, my name is Eliza. I'll be your lady's maid. I've come to help you dress for dinner," she says eagerly.

"Oh, I see. I was not expecting a lady's maid. Do come in," I say, totally taken aback by her presence. *A lady's maid. He actually assigned me a lady's maid.* I have the sudden urge to pinch my skin again, but if I keep that up I will end up with red welts and bruises on my arms. And that would not be pretty. Eliza walks over to the dress lying on the bed. "Is this what my lady wishes to wear this evening?" she asks.

"It is. I hope it is appropriate," I say. I realize that Eliza will be a great asset for me. It's been a long time since I have had to act like a lady. She will be my guide and of course she can help me dress appropriately, making sure that I always look respectable for the Master. *Oh my, I just called him Master!"*

Eliza helps me dress for dinner. I have to admit that I find it a bit uncomfortable having another woman dress me. I mean, I am not helpless; I have been dressing myself for many years. But I haven't been wearing dresses like this, either, with all the accessories that go with them.

Jax has thought of everything. Not only do I have a stockpile of dresses, he has provided me with undergarments, corsets, stockings, and shoes. I feel like a fairy princess being dressed for the king. As Eliza works my hair into a sultry style, I stare at my image in the mirror. *Who is this woman before me?* I no longer look like a whore. Eliza has turned me into a stylish woman. A lady. It's only my first day here and already I am wondering how I am ever going to go back to Whitechapel when this agreement is over.

Eliza finishes with a slight bow and exits my room. I take one more glance at myself in the mirror and take a deep breath. It's time to face the Master. The butterflies in my stomach begin to flutter as the anticipation of seeing him again consumes me. I leave my room and slowly walk down the hallway. I am not used to wearing such elaborate shoes and I am finding it difficult to walk in them. I reach the top of the stairs and pray that I don't fall as I descend. I glance down into the foyer. Standing in full formal dress and gazing up at me is Jax. He's beautiful and again I find myself wondering how I ended up here. His gray eyes lock on me and he nods with approval. His smile is all the encouragement I need and I slowly and gracefully begin to descend the stairs. He waits for me at the bottom of the stairs, his eyes never leaving me. When I get to the bottom, he holds out his arm.

"Shall we?" he asks.

I take my hand and rest it on his arm as he escorts me to the dining room.

The dining room is very large, with a long dining table that looks as if it could seat at least twenty people, if not more. I don't take the time to count, but there are many chairs that line both sides of the table. On the far side of the room, there is a fireplace with a roaring fire blazing. The room is warm and toasty, and the fireplace, along with the lit candles on the dining table, put the room into a romantic glow. It's like a fairytale. I feel like Beauty from the French fairy tale *Beauty and the Beast*. However, I don't think that Jax is a beast. He's a handsome prince—and for now, until he tires of me, he's my prince.

Jax has not spoken to me since he greeted me at the stairs and I find myself curious as to his thoughts. When he looks at me, he looks as if he wants to devour me, but he is always so restrained and collected. He leads me to the end of the table, pulls out a chair, and gestures for me to sit. I nod and obey. As he pulls in my chair, he leans down and kisses me right behind my ear and says, "You look beautiful tonight." And there it is, that prickly and tingling feeling that consumes my body every time he gets close to me.

"Thank you," I reply, breathless.

He takes the seat at the head of the table, directly to my right. Once he sits, his footmen begin serving our meal, course by course. At first I think that we are going to eat our meal in silence. I could say something and break the silence, but I get the feeling that I should wait until I am spoken to before I speak. There is something very commanding and domineering about Jax that puts me in a constant state of submission.

After several minutes of silence, Jax asks, "So, my dear, did you have any trouble today?"

"Trouble?" I ask, hoping he will clarify his meaning. I have a feeling he is referring to trouble with Joe, but I don't want to assume.

"Yes, you were worried last night that the man you're living with might not accept our little arrangement," he explains.

I lower my eyes. "He forbade me to come to you. I usually do as Joe asks—within reason, that is—but by my presence here, I've obviously defied him."

"For me?" he asks, surprised.

"Of course. And, well ... the money is a pretty good incentive as well," I reply honestly.

He chuckles. "You are blunt, aren't you?"

"I'm sorry if I offended you. I don't believe in deceit; not in my real life. I know that sounds like a contradiction, but I spend my evenings being whatever the man I am with wants me to be. It is a world full of deceit and I do it because I have no choice. You have allowed me to be myself. You never saw that side of me and with my being here, so I believe it is fair to assume that you accept me for who I am."

"Well said, my dear. I truly admire your honesty," he replies.

I add, "And if I told you that I was here because I was madly in love with you, well ... forgive me, Jax, but you would know that I was lying."

He chuckles again. "I think I have made an excellent choice in choosing you, Marie."

"If I may add one thing? Money aside, Jax, I really want to be here. I feel ..."

"Go on," he encourages. "Tell me what you feel, Marie."

"I ... well ... I feel a connection with you. My body reacts to your presence alone and I find that fascinating. That has never happened to me before and I just couldn't pass up the opportunity to know you better."

He smiles and reaches over and touches my hand. Taking his finger and stroking my hand with featherlike touches, he says, "I know what you mean. I feel the same and the feeling is foreign to me as well."

I smile, because I feel that I have pleased him. I am surprised at the gratification that it affords me, but pleasing him is all I find myself wanting to do.

We continue to eat our meal and then he asks, "So, you have met Jasper?"

"Yes, he collected me from Whitechapel earlier this afternoon. He was waiting for me exactly where you had said."

"Good. He will be your personal coachman while you are here with me. Anytime during the day you wish to go anywhere, Jasper will take you and remain with you at all times. He is not only your coachman, but also your protector."

"Protector?" I ask. "Why on earth would I need a protector?"

"Yes, Marie, a protector. For the time being, you belong to me. And while you are mine, you fall under my protection."

"But what are you protecting me from?" I ask.

"My dear, there are many evils in this world. Many evils from which a beautiful woman like you needs protection. Not to mention that we have a killer on the loose in Whitechapel. I assume you will be returning back to your home during your afternoons and I want to make sure you are safe. You may think of me as being overprotective, but I have my reasons."

Oh, Mary Nichols. I had almost forgotten. "Reasons?" I ask.

"Let's just say that a long time ago I made the mistake of leaving a woman alone. I will never do that again."

After dinner, Jax thanks the footman and passes his compliments to the cook. He gets up from his chair and steps over to me. He pulls out my chair and reaches for my hand. I take it as I rise from my seat and he escorts me from the dining area. As we walk through the house, we encounter Rothschild.

"We are retiring," he says to Rothschild. "Please have the brandy stocked in my private sitting room."

"Yes sir," Rothschild says and hurries off.

Jax leads me up the grand staircase and we turn toward my room. When we get down to the end of the hallway he says, "I hope you find your room comfortable?"

"I do. It is lovely. Unlike anything I have ever imagined," I reply.

"Good." He pauses at the doorway and then opens my door and we step inside. "That door leads to my bedchamber."

"I wondered about that earlier. I tried to open it, but it was locked."

"Yes. When you are here, it will remain open. You are allowed to enter my bedchamber at any time you wish. On the other side of my bedchamber is my private sitting room. It is where I spend most of my time in the evenings. You are also allowed to enter that room at your will. You can get there by going through my bedchamber, or using the doors across the hallway from this room."

Just then I realize that we are not alone as Eliza steps into view. "Thank you," I reply, a bit embarrassed that she has overheard our conversation and the access to Jax's bedchamber that I have been granted. I really don't know why this bothers me, I am a prostitute for God's sake, but somehow, being here makes me feel different.

"I think we should perhaps talk. I know you are wondering what I expect of you and I really need to make myself clear. You may freshen up if you wish—perhaps you would like to dress in something more comfortable? I am sure that Eliza will help you with anything you need. Then, when you are done, I want you to join me in the sitting room. But do not take long, I am not a patient man."

"Yes sir, I would like that. I shall not be long at all."

He reaches for my hand and brings it to his lips. "I will see you soon, then."

He steps out of my room and closes the door behind him. I turn to face Eliza and find her searching through my things. She turns to face me with a beautiful dressing gown in her hands. "Shall my mistress wear this?" she asks.

"Oh yes, Eliza, that would be lovely," I reply.

She hurriedly helps me from my formal dress and helps me into the dressing gown, then brushes out my hair. Never in all my life have I felt so pampered.

Pleased with the result, I say, "Thank you, Eliza, that will be all for tonight."

"As you wish, miss. I shall return in the morning."

"Thank you." She puts the brush down and walks to the door. As she is about to leave, she turns back to me and says, "If I may, Miss Marie: I have seen many women come and go from this room, but I have never seen my Master so taken with any of them as he is with you." She turns back to the door, steps out, and closes it behind her.

Even though her words make me happy, I can't help but feel jealousy toward all the women before me. I mean, I always knew that I would not have been the only woman in this man's life. How could I be? But hearing it confirmed causes a pang of jealousy and insecurity in the pit of my stomach. A wave of fear rushes over me. If I step into that sitting room, there is no turning back. I could leave now, run back to Joe, and beg his forgiveness. At least with Joe I will not suffer a broken heart. I know that if I proceed with the course that I am on, my heart is at a terrible risk. But suddenly Eliza's words come back to me: *I have never seen my Master so taken with any of them as he is with you.*

I find her words soothing; they give me the courage to see this through. If I don't, I will spend the rest of my life wondering about what could have been. That is a terrible way to live.

Feeling better, I step through the door that was locked earlier and into Jax's bedchamber. The dark woods and the jeweled fabric tones in rich velvet give the room an intoxicating, masculine appeal. Jax is not here; I assume that he is already in the sitting room, waiting for me. I cross the length of the large room to the door on the other side, leading to his private sitting area. I turn back to take in his bedchamber, resting my eyes on the large, wooden four-poster bed that takes over the room with its presence and realize that there is no other place I would rather be, my broken heart be damned.

Stepping into the sitting room, I find Jax sitting on the settee, a drink in hand. It appears that he is reading the post. He looks very comfortable; he is still wearing his trousers, but the suspenders are loosened. His shirt is loosened from his pants and unbuttoned halfway down. It's odd seeing him in such a state of undress, but I'm not complaining. He looks downright sexy; I could stare at him like this for hours. When he realizes that I have stepped into the room, he looks over at me and gestures for me to sit down next to him.

"I'm pleased to see that you made yourself comfortable. I want you to remember that when we are in these rooms, your comfort is of the utmost importance."

"Thank you," I say as I sit down next to him.

He takes his hand and gently strokes it along my cheek. Pausing on my cheekbone briefly, his fingers travel to my lips. Caressing my lips with his fingers, he says, "I want to kiss you."

Exhaling the breath I didn't realize I was holding, I reply, "I want you to kiss me."

"That pleases me, but first I think I need to be clear as to what I expect of you."

"The rules?" I reply.

"You called them rules, Marie. I look at them as expectations." He pauses briefly until he is sure that he has my undivided attention and then continues, "As I stated last evening, I want you here by six every evening. You are free to move about town during the day, but from six in the evening until six in the morning you are mine. Understood?"

I nod. "Understood."

"You will not entertain any other men while you are with me. We are exclusive."

"Does that mean that you will not entertain any other women?"

"That's exactly what it means." I smile because to my surprise, that pleases me. He then continues, "We will dine together and retire to this room every evening. What happens beyond that is up to you."

"Me?"

"I will never make you do anything you don't want to do. And in most cases, you will have to tell me what you want from me. I envision us having a very sensual relationship, Marie, but I will not push that upon you. Do you understand what I am saying?"

"I'm not sure. Are you telling me that you will not have sex with me?"

"No, that's not what I am saying. I am saying that I will only have sex with you when you ask me to have sex with you. Everything that happens between us, you will request."

"Oh ..." I am in complete shock. My life is a series of men telling me what they want. *Get on your knees, Marie. Show me your ass, Marie. Spread your legs, Marie.* Is he really saying what I thinking he's saying? "Jax, may I be blunt?" He nods. "Are you telling me that if I do not want to have sex with you, or do anything of a sexual nature with you, I don't have to do it?"

"That's exactly what I am saying."

"And you will not be angry with me and send me back to Whitechapel?"

"That's correct."

"Then, if I may, why are you paying me?"

"Marie, now it's my turn to be blunt. I will not lie to you; my whole purpose of having you here, for paying you to be here, is so that I can ravage your body whenever I choose. However, I am not a man that takes what he wants from a woman. She has to give it to me willingly. I want you to want nothing more than to have me inside you. I want you to want to have my hands on your body. I want you to want my kisses. I want your body and your mind to hunger for me."

"Oh ..." I am breathless by his words. Just by him speaking them, he has achieved exactly what he wants. All I can think about is his kiss, his hands, and having him deep inside me. However, at this point I am unsure of what to say or do next. Do I just come out and tell him that I want to have sex with him? I squirm.

"What's wrong?" he asks.

"I've never told a man what I wanted."

"I know."

He leans in closer to me and nuzzles his nose close to my ear. His breath is hot on my neck and I am drunk with wanting him. "Say it, Marie," he whispers into my ear. "Tell me you want me."

Dizzy with lust, I reply, "I want you, Jax."

It was all I needed to say. Jax suddenly lifts me, carries me into his bedchamber, and sets me down next to his bed. Standing next to me, he asks, "What do you want, Marie?"

I thought I had already told him that. "I want you, Jax," I repeat.

"I know that, you've already told me. But what's next?"

Oh Lord, he wants me to guide him every step of the way.

He stands behind me, his right arm draped low across my middle, resting dangerously close to my private area. His left arm trails down the back of my neck, causing my insides to flutter. I lean my head back onto his shoulder and give him complete access to my neck. He whispers in my ear, "Tell me, Marie."

I realize that he means what he says and that he will not do more than tease me until I tell him exactly what I want. So, going against everything that I know, I beg, "Kiss me, Jax, please."

His lips are hot on my neck as he trails kisses from behind my ear to the base of my throat. When he returns back to my ear, he whispers, "Tell me more."

I am literally floating. All I can think about are his lips on mine. "Kiss me, Jax." He proceeds to kiss my neck again and I add, "No, not there," I say breathlessly.

He whispers, "Where?"

I turn my head toward him and say, "My lips." Before I can get my next breath out, his lips are crushing against mine. They are warm and soft and as he deepens the kiss, our tongues dance in the warm wetness of our mouths. I feel like I can't get enough of him and I don't ever want him to stop kissing me. He breaks the kiss and I can't help but frown at the loss.

Turning me around, he caresses my face and leans in to kiss me again, pulling me close against him. I can feel his erection pushing against my middle and the wetness pools between my legs.

Oh God, the passion that this man drives me to is unlike anything I have ever experienced before. As he continues to kiss me, I find myself clinging to him. It's as if I am trying to crawl inside him. He breaks our kiss, both of us breathing heavily.

"Make love to me, Jax. I need you" I plead.

He shakes his head. "You know I don't make love."

"Jax," I beg, "fuck me. Please."

"No."

"No?" *Is he fucking serious? He's got to be jesting with me, surely.*

"I think you have had enough tonight."

"But ... I thought we were doing what I want?"

"We are, but that does not mean I have to do everything you ask."

I frown. I'm so frustrated I could slap him. He brought me so close, he made me want him beyond reason, and then nothing. Absolutely nothing. "Why are you being so cruel?" I ask quietly.

"Oh, my beautiful Marie. I am not being cruel. We have all the time in the world. I want to savor our times together. I want you to lie in your bed tonight and dream of me. Dream about my kisses and my hands on your body caressing you. Dream, Marie, that I am buried deep inside you, giving you all the pleasure you deserve. I want you to wake in the morning, your first thought of me, desperate to have me."

Though mesmerized by his words, I am at a loss. Never in all my days have I encountered a man like this, a man with such control and restraint. It makes me wonder what kind of man I am quickly falling in love with.

He kisses me on the cheek and turns back toward the door. I do as I am told and head off to bed. And as I walk toward my room, I know I will do everything that he said I would do. I will dream about him in explicit detail; the only thing I want is him.

Chapter Six

September 3, 1888

I wake the next morning with a start. *Where am I?* Glancing around the bedroom, memories of last night flood my mind. I am no longer in Whitechapel, in the dismal flat in which I live, and I am definitely not sleeping on the cot I call a bed. No, I am in Jax's home, in this luxurious room, snuggled under down and satin and feeling like a queen. *How did I get here?* I wonder.

Stretching my arms, I pull the covers up close and giggle. *This really isn't a dream.* I lie there for several minutes, enjoying my surroundings, until there is a knock at the door. Holding the covers up close, I say, "Come in."

To my surprise, it's Eliza. "What shall my mistress wear today?" she says as she walks over to the wardrobe and begins to rustle through the dresses hanging there. She is in a bubbly mood today and her smile is infectious.

"I really didn't give it much thought. Why don't you pick something for me?" I reply. I love the idea of not having to make any decisions.

"As you wish." Several minutes pass before Eliza walks over to the bed with a very pretty blue frock. As she lays the frock on the bed, she says, "The Master loves blue."

I definitely think I will be wearing more blue in the future.

A couple of hours later, I am bathed, dressed, and coiffed as much as I can be. Eliza tells me that I can breakfast in the dining room and leaves with a curtsey as I thank her. I wonder if Jax is awake. When I look out my window and see that the sun has fully risen, I realize that it is later than I thought. I'm sure that Jax has already emerged from his bedchamber, but I decide to check anyway. I knock on the door adjoining our rooms, but there is no answer. Turning the knob, I quickly find out that the door is locked. *Curious,* I think to myself. *I thought he said that these rooms would remain open and that I could come and go as I please.*

Since I cannot get in the room, I decide to make my way to the dining room. I assume that Eliza meant the same room in which we ate dinner last evening, so I make my way in that direction. When I walk into the dining area, I see that there is nobody here. *Perhaps I have the wrong room.* I step out into the hallway and walk back toward the foyer. Rothschild is walking toward me.

"Can I help you, miss?" he asks.

"Forgive me, Eliza said that I could breakfast in the dining room, but I just came from there and it is empty. I must have come down too late."

"Oh no, miss, Eliza forgot to differentiate between the two dining rooms. The room you dined in last evening was the formal dining room. We also have a day room, where we breakfast and luncheon. Allow me." He gestured for me to follow him as he guided me toward my morning meal.

I will need a map of this house if I am ever to find anything besides my bedchamber.

After I finish my breakfast, I linger in the day room for more time than is necessary. I am really unsure of what to do with myself. Looking over at Rothschild, who stands against the wall while I remain at the table, I ask, "Rothschild, will Jax be joining me this morning?"

He shakes his head and replies, "No, miss, he will most likely be gone for the remainder of the day. I expect him to return before dinner."

I am disappointed that he is gone. I was really hoping to see him this morning. Thinking about all the things I could do this afternoon to occupy my time, I decide that it's probably best that I return to Whitechapel. I'm feeling uneasy about the way I left things with Joe and I really do need to make amends. I also need to make sure I have a home to return to when this arrangement is over. "Rothschild, could you have Jasper prepare the carriage for me? I should like to leave within the hour if that is doable."

"Of course, Miss Marie. I will talk to him directly," he replies.

Living the way I have for most of my adult life has made me realize how much I took for granted the simple pleasures of the wealth of my youth. My father was a landowner and a gentleman. Growing up, we always had staff to tend to our needs. An odd feeling comes over me as I realize how easy it was for me to fall back into the old habits of my youth.

As I instructed, forty minutes later the carriage was waiting for me out front, with Jasper standing proudly by the door awaiting my arrival. When he spots me, he quickly opens the carriage door and takes my hand to guide me inside. Once inside, he leans in and says, "Where to, miss?"

"Whitechapel, please," I reply.

"Any place in particular, miss?" he asks.

"My flat." I notice a slight frown on his face, but he quickly turns and proceeds to his post to drive the carriage.

When we arrive outside my building, Jasper stops the carriage, gets down from his post, and comes around and opens the door for me. He grasps my hand and helps me from the carriage. There are many people hustling and bustling about on Commercial Street this time of day. Those that I know look at me curiously.

As I begin walking toward my flat, Julia and Mrs. Harvey approach me. I've worked with both these ladies now for a couple of years and I can confidently say that I consider them good friends.

"My goodness, Marie, where did that come from?" Julia asks.

I hesitate. I am not sure how much information Jax wants me to divulge and I think it is best to err on the side of caution and not say too much. I reply airily, "There you go again, Julia, being a busybody, like always."

Ignoring my insult, she exclaims, "And look at that gorgeous dress you're wearing!"

"There is no need to worry your pretty little head with my transportation options or my wardrobe, Julia."

"But Marie, that carriage screams money! And the dress ..." She pauses and then adds, "You've got a new client, don't ya?"

"Julia, I am not at liberty to say right now. I think it would be best that you pretend that you didn't see me. At least not today," I say.

Perhaps coming to Whitechapel was a bad idea. But if I can get to Joe and hopefully find him in a better mood, perhaps I can go back to Jax with a clear conscience. Or perhaps I am just fooling myself; my mind and body will constantly betray Joe. I know without a shadow of doubt that I will stay with Jax as long as he wants me.

"Well aren't you the snooty one! Look at little miss high-and-mighty now with her fancy carriage and blue dress. She doesn't have time for her lower-class friends anymore!"

When I don't reply, she just glares at me while Mrs. Harvey tugs at her arm to go. But before she walks away, she throws one last dig at me: "I pity the one you're using now for your personal gain, Marie. You're a user, Marie! Always have been and always will be!" As Julia stomps off, Mrs. Harvey looks at me wearily as if to apologize for Julia's outburst and then trails behind her.

I really hated to be rude to two people that I call my friends, but I didn't want to give away too much information. Jax never made it clear to me what could and could not be told about our arrangement. I make a note to myself to be sure to ask him about it when I see him later.

Turning from the ladies walking away from me, I begin to walk toward my flat. *Hopefully Joe will be home and we can talk. Then I can put this uneasy feeling I have to rest.*

Who am I trying to kid? The only reason why I am back here to clear my conscience; so that I feel no guilt in leaving a man who has done nothing but take care of me over the last year. I know I'm a callous, selfish woman. It will be the end of me someday. But not today.

Walking through the door, I find the flat empty. It's not hard to determine that Joe is not here, the flat is only one room. I sit down in the chair and think, *Now what do I do?* I could always go down to the pub and see if he's there. But if I do that, then there will definitely be more questions from friends seeking answers I don't have.

I have a little time before I have to be back. Perhaps if I wait a while, Joe will return and we will have a chance to talk. Sitting at the table, I stare at the walls. I realize for the first time that this place is a dump. The paint is chipped in many places and peeling in others. I have lived here so long that I never really took notice of my surroundings; I was just thankful that I at least had a roof over my head, even though it leaked in many places. I was fortunate. Many who lived in the district didn't have the luxuries that I had afforded, if that is what you want to call them. Having a semi-dry place to sleep and a place to call home was once a luxury to me, but it is quite a contrast to Jax's home. I know that I have only been there one night, but I want the amenities that a life with Jax would provide. I want it so bad I can taste it.

I spend as much time as I can waiting for Joe, but he never returns. I really need to get back as it is quickly approaching six.

Leaving the flat, I head down to the curb where Jasper is patiently standing just outside the carriage. He smiles when he sees me. Many onlookers stare at me as I approach and Jasper helps me inside. Coming around to the window, he asks, "Home, Miss Marie?"

Home ... I like the sound of that. "Yes, Jasper, thank you."

I'm so proud of you for standing up to your so-called friend. You're a very strong woman and you belong to me! Always.

I arrive home with just enough time to dress for dinner. I rush to my room and find Eliza waiting for me. She helps me dress, straightens my hair, and applies some rouge to my cheeks.

"Forgive me for saying, miss, but you're looking a little pale. Are you feeling well?" Eliza asks.

I hadn't noticed it until she mentioned it, but my reflection does look a little pale. I reply, "I feel fine, Eliza. Perhaps being out and about today is taking its toll on me. It was a little warmer today than it has been recently. Perhaps the heat has blanched my cheeks." Just as I say that, I realize that I also have not eaten a thing today since breakfast. I am famished.

"Well, as long as you are feeling alright. This rouge will give your cheeks some color." As she works her magic, I watch her in the mirror. She really does know what she is doing. "There, miss, you look lovely. The Master will never know."

"Thank you, Eliza. I'm not used to having someone attend to me. I hope you know how much I appreciate all you do."

"Aw, go on, miss."

"Truly."

"Thank you, Miss Marie." She pauses and then says, "Look at the time! The Master will be waiting for you."

I quickly rise from the vanity and make my way to the dining room. Just as Eliza said, Jax is standing in front of the window on the other side of the room looking out, his back to me. "Jax?" I ask.

He turns and says, "Ah, Marie. There you are. I was beginning to worry."

"I'm sorry that I'm late. It won't happen again," I reply.

"Actually, my pet," he says, looking at his timepiece, "you are one minute early." I smile because I know how important punctuality is to him and again, I feel as if I have pleased him.

He walks over to the same chair I occupied last evening and slides it out. "Please sit," he says. I do as I am told and he slides my chair back in, moving me closer to the table.

"Thank you," I say demurely as he pulls out his own chair and proceeds to sit down.

"Did you have a good day?" he asks.

"I did, thank you," I reply.

"Jasper tells me that he took you to Whitechapel today, to your flat."

"He did," I reply.

"Did you return for a specific reason?" He pauses and then adds, "Before you respond, let me warn you, I will know if you lie to me. I abhor liars and expect nothing but honesty from you. Do not ever try to hide the truth from me." His voice is stern, almost sinister.

Where did that come from? He has never sounded like that with me before. For a brief moment, a sense of fear washes over me. But then his expression softens and he smiles at me, waiting for me to reply. "I was feeling bad about the way I left things with Joe yesterday and thought that if I went back, perhaps I would have the opportunity to talk to him about our arrangement."

"And did you?" he asks.

"No, I'm afraid not. He wasn't there when I arrived and I waited all afternoon for him to return, which he did not. I knew I was expected to be back here by six, so when I knew I was running out of time, I left."

"Did you converse with anyone else while you were there?" he asks.

I think for a moment and then remember speaking with Julia. "Actually, when I arrived I was approached by a friend."

"A male or female friend?"

"Female."

"And what did she say?"

"Well, she was quite surprised by the carriage that I arrived in. As you know, most people in the district are not used to seeing wealthy people around. She had a lot of questions."

He looks at me curiously and then says, "What kind of questions?"

"Well, she wanted to know where I got such a fancy carriage. And she speculated about the wealth behind it. Oh, and she made a comment about my dress."

"And what did you tell her?"

I was afraid that his line of questioning would lead us here. I pray that I gave her the correct response. I reply, "Well, I made a joke about her being a busybody and when she pushed, I basically told her that I was not at liberty to say and that it would be best if she forgot she saw me today."

"I see," he replies thoughtfully.

"I hope I said the right thing. You never really made it clear to me as to what I could or could not say about our arrangement."

"No, I did not. But you passed with flying colors."

"Excuse me? I passed?" I ask. *Is he testing me?*

"Yes, you passed. I didn't set up the conversation with your friend, but I purposely didn't tell you what you could or could not divulge. I knew there would be questions when you returned to Whitechapel and I wanted to see how you would handle it on your own. You must understand, I like my privacy and you did well to preserve it. Well done. I think I will reward you tonight."

I am smiling from ear to ear. I have pleased him again and that makes me very happy. *Reward me?* I wonder what he means by that, but I think it is better not to ask and just let him surprise me.

And so, just as we did last evening, we finish our dinner and retire to his personal sitting room.

He sits in the chair across from me and studies me curiously. I feel very intimidated by his wolfish gaze, and I think that maybe it would be acceptable to ask him why he is staring, but I do not. Suddenly I think that he is finally going to do more with me than feed me and talk to me.

He gets up from his chair and walks over and stands before me. "Come," he commands as he holds out his hand for me to take. I do as he asks, his hand in mine as he leads me to the door to his bedchamber. Before he gets to the door, he stops and turns toward me. "I will not hurt you."

What an odd thing to say, I think to myself. I have been with hundreds of men, all very different. Some liked it slow and sensual, while others liked it rough and bruising. The worst were the ones that were trying to prove a point to me, themselves, or some arbitrary being they felt they needed to answer to. Yes, those were the worst experiences of my life. The last one I had like that nearly beat me to death, just to prove that he could take from me whatever he wanted and hit me as hard as he pleased. He held so much anger and unleashed all that pent-up nastiness on me. But he wasn't the only one. There were others. When I would encounter one of those, usually I could not work for the next day or two. When I would arrive at Madame Grace's every evening, I always wondered what type of arse I would get. But with Jax, the last thing on my mind was that he might hurt me.

He looks at me quizzically and asks, "Did you hear me?"

"Ah, yes. But honestly, Jax, that was the last thing on my mind."

"Perhaps, but I wanted you to know that," he replies.

He doesn't give me the chance to respond as he steps closer to me. His breath caresses my face. As his lips come closer to my own, his words replay in my head. *I won't hurt you. I won't hurt you.* Although I have no fear of him hurting me, something inside tells me that I need to remember those words one day.

Before I inhale my next breath, his lips land on mine. The world begins to spin out of control as his lips, wet and moist, join with mine. As he feathers kisses on my lips, he takes his tongue and slowly grazes my bottom lip, causing me to open my mouth. This gives him the perfect opportunity to invade my mouth. Once his tongue slips in, my neck arches toward him of its own volition as my body presses against him. I'm sinking into an ocean of pure bliss. My body tingles as his lips slowly devour mine. I have been waiting for him to kiss me, touch me, and devour me since I ran into him in the alleyway three nights ago. I am desperate for him. I want everything from him and the passion that he affords me in this one kiss is enough to ignite a fire deep in my belly. My arms reach up to encircle his neck and he quickly steps away. Suddenly I am cold and bereft.

"Do you like to be kissed, Marie?" he asks.

I look at him curiously. *Did I not show him that I liked his kiss?* A little dazed, I reply, "Yes, I do." *Why would he ask such a thing? Could he not feel the heat between our bodies? Am I the only one who felt the connection between us?*

"Have any of the men you've been with kissed you like I do?"

Shaking my head, I reply, "No. Most of the men I have been with do not kiss me. They are not interested in the gentler side of sex."

"The gentler side?" he asks. "A kiss is not always gentle, Marie. A kiss can be bruising. Surely you know that."

"I ... I ... wouldn't know." I am beginning to feel like this is my first time with a man. I have to laugh at myself. Despite where I've been and what I've done with so many men, the kiss he just gave me is my first real kiss. Even my husband hadn't kissed me like this. He kissed me, yes, but his kisses were wet and sloppy. He was not an experienced lover. I believe that if Jax and I have sex tonight, it will be my first time having a real sexual experience.

"Do you want me to kiss you again?" he asks, staring into my eyes. His gray eyes are sultry and demanding.

Breathlessly, I reply, "Yes."

He steps toward me. Our breaths mingle together and my body begins to feel the tingling of his close proximity again. His hand cups my cheek as he comes closer to my lips. His tongue teases my mouth as he slowly coaxes me to open for him. I do not protest. I do what his tongue asks me. At first he is warm and gentle, just like the first kiss, but then the kiss changes as our bodies fall together. His lips become demanding, devouring and so strong against my own.

His hands move away from my face and reach to the back of my neck, grasping at my hair as he kisses me harder. My hands are still at my side, as I am afraid to reach up and touch him again. When I did that earlier, he stepped away from me and that is the last thing I want.

Every essence of control drains from my body. As his lips press hard against mine, bruising the tender skin that covers them, I give in to his silent demands. In that moment, I realize that this man owns me. I do not know how or why, but I am his. With all my control gone, my arms reach up to his neck and I pull his body against mine. I can feel his erection against my core as he masterfully manipulates my mouth to bend to his will. I am lost.

Pulling away breathlessly, he asks, "Can you feel it, Marie?" He pants and then adds, "Can you smell it?"

At first I am not sure what he is asking me. I'm feeling a lot of things right now ... and then I realize what he means by the smell. The room smells like sex and it is because there is a puddle of wetness between my legs. *Oh God, I am so embarrassed!*

"The human body is fascinating," he says casually, as if the smell in the room doesn't bother him. "I will never get enough of the sensations the body goes through when it prepares for sex." He stops and I am sure he sees the mortification on my face.

"Oh Marie, don't be embarrassed. It is incredibly sexy and arousing. Honest." He moves in closer and then whispers, "Let me show you."

I am at a loss for words as he takes me under his spell again. This man is a drug worse than opium. He is my addiction. As he bends to kiss me again, he hisses, "I want you." And as his tongue slides leisurely along my bottom lip, I am totally at his mercy. I want him too. I crave him. He consumes me. I have never felt this wanton need with a man before. Never.

"Come," he says as he directs me toward the door and we enter his bedchamber. *This is really going to happen,* I think to myself. He guides me to the bed and slowly unties my dressing gown and lets it drop to the floor. He then unties the bodice of my nightdress and then pushes it off and down my shoulders. It falls to the floor like a pillow of silk and lace. I am left standing in my combination knickers. The pink satin tickles my skin as Jax steps back and stares at me.

"You're lovely," he says. His gray eyes grow dark as he walks around me and I realize that I am on display for his approval. He is like a wolf circling his prey, testing my resolve.

Is he waiting to see what I will do? I'm in such a haze of passion and desire, I do nothing. My body is so attuned to him that all I can do is patiently await his next command.

He takes his hand and lightly touches my cheek, dropping to my neck and then runs it down across the swell of my breasts. My nipples instantly pucker at his touch. Moving to stand behind me, he begins stroking my spine with the lightest of touches. My body is so sensitive to his every touch, every breath ... I feel drunk on passion.

"Have you ever been with a man, Marie?"

What? He knows what I am, he's paying me to be here ... why would he ask such a thing? I reply hesitantly, "Jax, you know ..."

Before I can finish, he cuts me off. "That's not what I asked you." He stares down at me. "I don't want to know about those idiots who have paid you 4d to touch you and fumble between your legs until they get off prematurely. They aren't men. I'm talking about a man who knows how to pleasure a woman. A man who will put your needs first. A man who will only reach his pleasure after you have reached yours." He pauses and then continues, "So, Marie, I will ask you again. Have you ever been with a man?"

"I ... I ..." He makes it very difficult for me to speak as his face comes in closer to my ear. He places tender kisses behind my ear and down my neck.

Nuzzling close to my ear, he says, "Tell me, Marie, do they make you feel like this?"

His words are my undoing and my body loses all control. My legs are weak and I am having difficulty standing. My center of gravity is gone, my equilibrium off balance. As I began to collapse, he catches hold of me and sweeps me up into his strong arms. I am cascading on a wave of pleasure from just his words and featherlike touches that tease my skin. His kisses consume me. I feel wanton and needy and I know I will never get enough of him. He will give and give, but I will always want more.

He gently lays me down on the bed and says, "Answer me, Marie."

Straining to get my breath back to speak coherently, I reply in a whisper, "No, I have never been with a real man."

"And have those fools that you have been with before made you feel like I do?" he asks, his tone demanding an answer.

"No, none of them have made me feel like this," I whisper.

"Now, Marie, tell me what you are feeling," he demands.

How on earth do I answer that? How do I articulate to him the many emotions and sensations that are coursing through my body?

When I don't answer right away because I am trying to find the words, his patience runs out. He says, "When I ask you a direct question, Marie, I expect an answer. I will only ask one more time. What are you feeling?"

"I'm not avoiding your question. I'm struggling to put all the feelings I'm having right now into words. One minute I am floating on a cloud and the next I'm on the precipice of sensations that are consuming my body. These sensations give me pleasure unlike anything I have experienced before. My body is an instrument and you its maestro. What I'm feeling, what you make me feel, is something I have never felt before."

"Good girl. And tell me, Marie, who do you belong to?"

The answer to this question is perfectly clear to me. I don't hesitate as I answer with conviction, "You, Jax. I belong to you."

"That's my girl." He cups my chin with his hand, tilting my face so that I am looking directly into his eyes. His thumb grazes my bottom lip and I shudder as he leans in closer.

Oh please, kiss me again, I silently beg. I am disappointed when his lips land on my neck instead of my lips, but my disappointment fades quickly as he leaves kisses along my neck and across my collarbone. I'm writhing in pleasure, my pussy throbbing to be touched and stroked—anything to provide me with the release I so desperately need. He does nothing to relieve my discomfort and only continues to tease me.

"You don't have to be afraid, I won't hurt you."

There it is again. Why does he think that I am afraid that he'll hurt me? Looking into his eyes, unable to find the words, I say silently, *Jax, remember, I belong to you. I'm your willing captive and I have no fear of you or what's to come.*

He kisses me as if he can read my thoughts. His lips are velvety soft and gentle. His breath is hot on my mouth and I hungrily inhale, desperate to take as much of him as I can. I let out a soft moan when he whispers, "Unless you want me to." He smiles at me with a devilish grin as I realize what he just said.

What is he trying to tell me?

Is he trying to scare me? Is he trying to make me run, to doubt him? Maybe this isn't a good idea, this arrangement of ours. I should collect the clothes I arrived in and leave. But he knows as well as I do that I won't run, not now, not ever. I am his captive, his prisoner. I am his.

His eyes sweep down my body as I lie on his bed. When his eyes reach mine, his grin turns sinister. For the first time since I have been with him, something inside of me tells me I should fear him, but I can't. Before I can speak, he's on top of me, his hands roaming all over my body as his lips again meet mine. His touch becomes urgent, demanding. He rips the remainder of my clothes from my body in one fell swoop. The pretty pink knickers lie in shreds all around me on the bed.

Seizing me into his grasp, he takes my breath away with a hard, bruising kiss. I gasp as he climbs on top of me, gripping my hips. His hands are strong and determined. He presses his weight down, constricting my chest, and I begin to panic. I can't breathe. I begin to struggle and he becomes wild. The more I struggle the more he kisses and nips at my body. He eases his weight on my body slightly and I gasp for air. I feel like I'm about to fall into a fit or something when his lips begin to trail along my jawline and down to my neck. He kisses and licks me, allowing his teeth to graze my skin, and I begin to relax.

His breathing is heavy as he takes his left hand and trails it along my body to my core. His fingertips graze my clit and I'm on fire. I've been silently begging him for this and now he is teasing me in the spot I need him most. As he moves his hands back up my body, I groan in frustration. He looks down at me and grins. Once his hand meets my bare breast, he strokes my nipple. Bringing his mouth down, he sucks and my nipple puckers in response. His hand begins to slowly move back down my body and I already begin to anticipate his touch. He continues to suck on my breast as my back arches and a moan escapes me, the jolt of pleasure tears through my insides, begging him for more.

His hands roam all over my body, only breaking from my skin when he struggles to tug off his clothes. I realize in this moment that this is the first time I have seen in such a state of chaos. He's always been so controlled, refined ... but as the passion builds between us, I can see that he has lost his battle to remain that way. When he finally frees himself of his clothes, he sits back and regards me warily. I can't help but stare at his beautiful body. My imagination did not do him justice; his strong torso shows every muscle across his abdomen, defined and chiseled.

Suddenly, I am embarrassed at my nakedness. My knees close together and my hands shield my breasts. He says, "Never hide yourself, Marie. You have a beautiful body." My legs fall open at his words and he positions himself between them. On his knees in front of me, he grasps his cock and strokes it. The sight of him touching himself is my undoing.

"Please," I beg.

"Tell me what you want, Marie."

"I want you," I plead and my eyes drift closed.

"You have me. Open your eyes, Marie, and look," he says as he rubs the head of his cock against my clit. Tiny sparks of pleasure jolt through my body. He then pushes inside of me, covering my body with his. He pulls out before pushing back in again, moving agonizingly slow. He does this over and over again as erotic pleasure pulsates through my body.

As soon as he finds his rhythm, he positions my leg so that they are straight up, each leg resting on his respective shoulder. This allows him to penetrate deep inside me. He continues to thrust into me, going in hard and fast and pulling out frustratingly slow. I gasp. He does this again and again, taking me hard and making me feel every inch of his length as he slowly pulls out, only to thrust in hard again.

He is holding me so tightly, my breathing is impaired. I realize in this moment that for as much sex as I have had in the past, I have never actually had real sex. I know that makes absolutely no sense. But he was right; a real man has never fucked me—until now. He drives into me with purpose, as if his last breath depends on getting me off. He is so attuned to my needs; I have never had that before. He's going to spoil me. I will be ruined when I leave here. No man will ever compare to him. No man will ever measure up. No man will ever make me feel the way I do now.

With these thoughts, I explode. The pleasure I feel is unlike anything I have ever felt before. I cry out, arching my back as he finds his release. I can feel him pulsating inside me. My pussy is convulsing around him, greedily milking him for everything. I could stay like this forever ... but before I can have another thought, he's gone.

I feel like a cold bucket of water has been dumped on me. *Why would he pull away so quickly? Did I do something wrong?* My eyes look around the room, but I don't see him until I feel the bed shift in front of me. As he kneels between my legs, his tongue softly kisses me *there*.

Oh God, what is he doing? Jax, please stop!

You need to stop, Jax, please.

Please, Jax.

Oh God, Jax, don't stop. He slides his finger inside of me and begins pumping as he licks and sucks at my clit. The sight of his head between my legs is the most erotic thing I have ever seen. I moan and run my hand through hair as my orgasm rocks me to the core. He continues to pump and suck and I feel as if I am going to lose my mind.

As the sensations subside he's inside me again, thrusting deep. His lips find mine and he kisses me hard. I can taste myself on him, but I don't care. I find that I can't get enough of his kiss. That fact that his mouth was just *there* and now he's here kissing me is erotic.

He pulls back and grins. "You like tasting yourself on me, don't you?" he asks.

I know it's utterly sinful, but I answer with the only answer that comes to mind. "Yes," I say breathlessly. He kisses me again. He's panting as he thrusts into me, hard and determined. This time is different. He's not so much about taking his time, torturing me with pleasure. This time he is desperate, showing no mercy as he pushes himself to release. This time, it's not about pleasuring me, this time, it's all for him. I feel his body tense as he makes one final thrust and then he pulls out of me and begins to stroke himself until he comes all over my belly. *Holy fuck.*

He continues to stroke his cock while kneeling in front of me, ensuring that every drop is expelled. This man, this sexual master who fine-tunes my body like a well-played symphony, mesmerizes me. I was in awe of the reserved and controlled man that I met in the alleyway, but I am totally and completely in love with the sexy, uninhibited man who just fucked me.

After he cleans me up he gets into bed next to me and pulls me close. Lying in his arms, I realize I can no longer be a prostitute. I can no longer sell my body to men I don't know. After tonight, this man, this beautiful man, owns me, body and soul.

I am his.

Chapter Seven

September 7, 1888

The next several days are basically a repeat of our first days together. We dine together every evening, retire to the sitting room, and then have wild and passionate sex. When I wake in the morning, he's always gone. I spend my afternoons in Whitechapel, which is where I am now. I really need to speak with Joe, but he is never home. I don't know why I feel the need to explain to him, I just really hate how we left things. After spending several days with Jax I know now I will never return to Joe. I can never return to this flat or Whitechapel. Maybe it is this sad news that I feel compelled to tell him. It will devastate him, but it is closure.

A frightening thought occurs to me: *What will I do when Jax tires of me? He's already told me that he would never fall in love with me. He's made that perfectly clear. Perhaps he will keep me long enough to earn enough money that I won't have to return to Whitechapel. But even if I did, I'd blow it all anyway. I'm a selfish person. I know my weaknesses. It will never happen.*

I spend another afternoon waiting for Joe, who never comes. As I sit in the chair in our flat, I begin looking through a stack of newspapers lying on the floor.

I pick up the oldest paper, dated September 4, and begin reading about a potential suspect in the Mary Ann Nichols murder. As I read further, I gasp. *Jack Pizer? I know this man!* Jack was sinister, evil, filthy, and always wore a leather apron. All the girls in the district referred to him as Leather Apron. Jack ran an extortion racket amongst the prostitutes. He demanded that we pay him money and if we didn't pay him a portion of our earnings he would use his fists until we handed over what he thought he deserved. We all knew that he was taking advantage of our circumstances and the fact that we were women. Many of us spoke with bravado about telling the authorities about him. But when it came down to it, we were all were afraid of him and what he'd do to us if we told, not to mention exposing ourselves to the police. I had heard many stories of how he would brutally beat those who did report him to the authorities. There are rumors that he beat one woman every day for a week and took all her money. Even Madame Grace was powerless; she once tried to speak for us but ended up with a few broken ribs and a black eye.

I made a point to steer clear of him most nights, but I did have a run in or two with him. He's a nasty man ... but to butcher a woman the way Mary Ann Nichols was butchered? I really don't know if that is something he could do. He's an opportunist and killing her would not get him any money.

The article continued on to say that the police decided that they had enough information to investigate Pizer and were searching for him. They hoped to find Nichols' killer or eliminate him as a suspect altogether. The last time he was seen was prior to Nichols' murder.

The September 5th newspaper has headlines that read, *Leather Apron – The Only Name Linked With The Whitechapel Murder*. Another story reads, *Strange Character Who Prowls About After Midnight*. I read more about Leather Apron and find that he is still at large and wanted for questioning by the Whitechapel police.

I pick up the next paper, dated September 6, and proceed to read that Mary Ann Nichols has been laid to rest at Little Ilford Cemetery. My thoughts drift back to that night, the night I met Jax. While a stranger was sweeping me off my feet, Mary Ann Nichols had been brutally murdered. As I play that night back in my head, I remember that the alley in which I ran into Jax was a direct link to

Buck's Row. *He was out of breath and I had assumed he had been running. Think, Marie! Where was he running from?* I stop for a moment and wonder. *Buck's Row! But why was he running? I had assumed that he was late for something, just like I was, but what if he wasn't? What if he was running from the murder scene?* I shook my head and admonished myself, *Oh Marie, you are being foolish and letting your imagination run away with you.*

As time ticks by, I realize that I have wasted another afternoon waiting for Joe. Perhaps I will not return to Whitechapel anymore.

I pick up the last paper in the stack, dated September 7, today's news. This paper states that the police are desperate to find Jack Pizer. They have not been able to catch up with him, and they have no other suspects. Mary Ann Nichols' murderer is still at large. The paper warns residents of Whitechapel to not go out after midnight because there is a killer on the loose. I toss the paper on the table. *Enough. I'm going back to Jax.*

I leave the flat, lock the door, and proceed down to the carriage where Jasper patiently waits for me. As I approach the carriage, I say, "Thank you for waiting. I'm sorry it took so long. We can go home now." *Home. I like the sound of that.*

Does she realize how beautiful she is?

After a nice dinner together and some casual conversation, Jax and I spend another evening together in unbridled passion. I have never slept as soundly as I do when I am in bed with Jax. I don't know if it is because I feel safe and comfortable in his bed or that I am just so sexually exhausted and sated that sleep is the only thing left for me to do. I am usually one that wakes several times during my sleep, mainly from fear of what might be entering my room, but that has not been the case since I have been with Jax. I have not had anything to be afraid of—until tonight.

September 8, 1888

In the wee hours of the morning, I wake with a start. I realize that I am breathing heavily and am sweating, my hands cold and clammy. I look over to Jax's side of the bed and see that he is not there.

"Jax?" I call for him but he doesn't answer. I get out of bed and proceed to the sitting room. Hopefully he is in there. After the way I have just woken up, I know that I don't want to be alone right now. For the first time since I have moved into Jax's home, I am fearful. I have no idea what has me so rattled, but it's the kind of terror that takes over your whole body.

When I get to the sitting room, I find it exactly as we left it when we went to bed. My dressing gown is thrown on the floor and Jax's waistcoat is draped over the chair. His half-empty brandy glass is still on the table. Nothing has moved or changed. *Where could he be?*

I want to go search the house, but it's so dark. Everyone has retired and I fear that I will get lost roaming through the house. So I go back to bed and wait for Jax to return. When the morning's light begins to creep into the room, I know that Jax is not in the house and I probably won't see him until this evening. I begin to worry.

Unable to find sleep again, I go back to my room where Eliza is waiting patiently for me to help me dress. After dressing I proceed downstairs to break my fast. I decide that I will not return to Whitechapel today and will instead try to amuse myself around the house. I find a pianoforte in the drawing room. Sitting down on the bench, I lay my hands on the keys. I used to be able to play many years ago, but as I stare at the keys I realize I remember nothing from those days. In my youth, I was an accomplished lady. I could draw, paint, and play the pianoforte. But it's all gone. Now, I'm just a whore. Frustrated, I get up and proceed to explore Jax's home. Anything to take my mind from the fears that plague me.

I find Jax's library and I am awestruck by the number of books that adorn the rich, dark wooden shelves. The smell of the paper and ink combined with the wood is intoxicating. I used to love to read when I was younger, when I lived with my parents. My life was much different then. In those days, I was a lady. I had forgotten how much I missed that life. Being here with Jax has made me remember many things from my past and what I have gone without over the years.

Perusing the shelves, I find Dickens' *David Copperfield*. I pull it from the shelf and proceed to the chair and begin to read:

CHAPTER I

I am born.

Whether I shall turn out to be the hero of my own life, or whether that station will be held by anybody else, these pages must show. To begin my life with the beginning of my life, I record that I was born (as I have been informed and believe) on a Friday, at twelve o'clock at night. It was remarked that the clock began to strike, and I began to cry, simultaneously.[ii]

I continue to read and realize many hours later that I have lost all track of time. That is, until Eliza comes bustling into the room. She says frantically, "Miss Marie, I have been looking everywhere for you. You must come quickly. You must dress for dinner. The Master will be home any minute now."

"Oh, I am sorry. I started reading and lost all concept of time." I then remembered that Jax had left in the middle of the night. "Has the Master returned?" I ask.

"No, not yet, but I expect him any minute. Now get a move on, you need to dress," she orders as she turns to leave the room. I quietly follow behind her.

Once I am dressed and ready for dinner, I proceed to the dining room. When I arrive, I immediately notice that there is only one place setting. *He's still not home—and by the looks of things, he's not coming home. Did I do something wrong?* His absence unnerves me. *Why would he just disappear without a word? Is he angry?* All sorts of insecurities run through my head, each one worse than the last. My stomach is in knots. Suddenly, I am no longer hungry.

"Rothschild, forgive me, but I don't think that I am very hungry. Please make my apologies to the cook."

"No apologies necessary, Miss Marie. I will instruct the cook to keep the meal warm for a while in case you change your mind."

"Thank you." I turn to leave and then stop. Turning back toward Rothschild, I ask, "Have you heard from Jax?"

"No, I have not," he replies.

Disappointed that he provides no answers to the questions running through my head, I nod and turn to leave. As I am leaving, he adds, "I would not worry, miss. The Master can be gone for days at a time. This is not the first time and I am sure that it will not be the last."

I stop at his words. "So he has done this before?"

"Yes, and he always returns."

"So you don't think something unfortunate has befallen him."

"No, miss, I do not," he replies. "I have been with the Master for a very long time. I am quite confident that he will return soon."

Feeling a little better by Rothschild's assurances, I thank him and leave the dining room. I am not tired and remember that I have a book that I was reading that I rather enjoyed. I had left the book in the library, so I decide to return and pick up where I left off.

When I return to the library I look on Jax's desk and see that the book I had left there is gone. The maid must have returned it to the shelf. I find the book on the shelves and pull it down, then begin to skim through until I find where I left off. Walking over to the chair, I sit and continue my story.

> *... There was one change in my condition, which, while it relieved me of a great deal of present uneasiness, might have made me, if I had been capable of considering it closely, yet more uncomfortable about the future. It was this. The constraint that had been put upon me, was quite abandoned.*[iii]

I smirk to myself. *Present uneasiness—yes, that is exactly what I have been feeling all day, a state of uneasiness.* Reading helped to get my mind off things earlier and so I let the book consume me. The hours tick by as I continue to lose myself in the book. Eventually I begin to grow tired, so I decide that I have read enough and that it is time to retire for the evening. Closing my book, I place it on the table in front of me and proceed to my room. It's pointless to sleep in Jax's bed tonight, so I stay in my own room.

Sunday comes and goes and Jax still has not returned home. I'm trying very hard to trust in Rothschild's assurances, but as time slips by, I feel lost and alone. I worry for his safety as well as my own. If he does not return, what shall become of me?

I've spent a lot of time reading the book I started a few days ago and now on Monday afternoon I find myself lost again in the words of Charles Dickens.

> CHAPTER 58
> *Absence*
> *It was a long and gloomy night that gathered on me, haunted by the ghosts of many hopes, of many dear remembrances, many errors, many unavailing sorrows and regrets.*[iv]

This book speaks to me; Copperfield is a character that I can relate to in so many ways. I find that he has suffered through many of the emotions that I have experienced over the last few days, as well as my entire life.

After an hour or so passes, a maid entering the room brings me back to the present. She carries a newspaper in her hand and I ask, "Is that today's news?"

"Yes miss, it is," she replies. She adds, "I bring the Master his paper every day. I am sorry to disturb you, I will just lay this on his desk and will be out of your way."

"You did not disturb me. May I see the paper?"

"Of course, miss, but please, leave it on the Master's desk when you are done."

She hands me the paper and I reply, "Thank you, I will."

Laying my book aside, I open up the paper. What I see brings shock and horror to my mind. *No, this cannot be! Not again!*

Another Murder in Whitechapel
Shocking Mutilation of the Victim

Once more, the neighborhood of Spitalfields has been terribly shocked by a brutal and mysterious murder.

Spitalfields! That's a small borough of Whitechapel and is not far from my home! I search the article to find out the name of the victim. Is it someone I know?

As I read through the article, I find out that her name is Annie Chapman. I did not know her personally, but I knew who she was and saw her on many occasions in the Ten Bells, drunk. She was of like profession, which does not surprise me. She was discovered at five minutes to six Saturday morning at 29 Hanbury Street. Her head was nearly severed from her body and the article said that she had further mutilations too gruesome to describe.

I put the paper down and think about the two women who have now been murdered. I realize that this killer is not going to stop. There will be more, of that I'm sure. Glancing down at the paper, I see another article that claims that Leather Apron had been brought in for questioning, but after his alibis checked out, he was released and was no longer considered a suspect. So, not only did another murder occur, the police were back to square one in their investigation.

I am horrified by what I've just read. How could someone mutilate another human being as this killer was doing to these women? I feel the need to escape this awful world and decide to go back to my book. I place the newspaper on Jax's desk, then sit down in the chair and open the book. Before I can start to read, the door flies open and Jax rushes in. He brushes right past me; I don't think he even sees me until he gets to his desk and turns.

The silent questions I want to ask him plague my mind, screaming. *Where were you? Why have you been gone for three whole days? What did I do that angered you so much that you had to leave? Talk to me!* But I don't utter one word of them aloud to him. I am afraid that his first words to me since his return are going to be that he's done with me and that he's sending me back to ensure my silence.

"I'm sorry for being in here," I say awkwardly. I've felt that his absence was because of something I had done wrong. And now I feel like I've gotten caught being somewhere I shouldn't be. Stumbling over my words, I continue, "I found a book on your shelf and was just reading."

"Marie, there is no need for you to apologize for being here. You are free to visit any room in this house that you wish. I told you from the beginning that as long as you sleep in this house, you will treat it as your own."

Oh ... "Well, I will get out of your way then," I reply.

"No, please stay," he says, then adds, "I'm sorry that I have been gone. Something came up that was out of my control and I simply couldn't avoid it. I didn't even have time to leave word with the staff that I would be gone. You must have been concerned, no?"

"I was concerned and worried. I thought perhaps that something horrible had happened to you or that I had angered you somehow."

He walks over to the chair and kneels down at my feet. "Oh, my beautiful pet, I could never be angry with you. You are the light in my rather dark world."

Oh ... His sultry voice, mixed with him kneeling before me, made me euphoric. Knowing that it wasn't me that kept him away makes me forget all the fears I had just a few hours ago. This man is my own personal drug that I am completely addicted to.

He looks down at the book that I am holding and says, "David Copperfield. Good choice."

"Thank you. I had never read anything by Charles Dickens before and this book called to me when I was perusing your shelves the other day. I have to admit, I am rather enjoying it. I can relate to Mr. Copperfield quite a bit."

He smirks. "I imagine so. But do not let his bleak life wear you down. Things are going to get better for you, I can assure you of that."

"Go on!" I reply. "How could you possibly know that?" I ask.

"Because I am the one that is going to change your life," he replies.

I am rendered speechless by his response. When he kisses my cheek and rises to turn away from me toward his desk, I know that he is not going to elaborate. He looks at me intently, silently begging me to trust him.

Trust him. I can do that. I think.

As he glances down at the papers, I can see that he is reading the same headlines that I had read a few minutes ago. "Another woman was murdered in Whitechapel," I say, stating the obvious as I know he just read this. But I feel the need to say something.

What happens next totally takes me by surprise. Jax takes the paper and throws it in the trash. He totally disregards the news story, he does not make any comment about it and storms from the room.

Was it something I said? Now what? Do I remain here and pretend that he didn't just do that, or do I go after him and find out what has him so upset? I think about this for several minutes and come to the conclusion that it would be in my best interest to remain here. My heart tells me to go after him, but my brain says to stay put. If he wanted me to know what had him so riled, he would have told me.

So I pick up my book like nothing happened and continue to read, although this time I can't concentrate on the book. I keep thinking about his reaction to the news and the murder. Anybody would react to such a story with horror and surprise. But Jax's reaction is anger and frustration, which is not how one would expect someone to react. *Except perhaps the killer ...*

No!

No, there is no way it could be Jax. He's kind and gentle. He fucks like a god, but that doesn't make him a killer. But wait ... the paper did say that the murder happened on Saturday. That was the first night Jax did not come home. Jax was gone. For three days! I gasp in horror. *No! I will not go there. Absolutely not!*

Frustrated that my mind is getting the best of me, I leave the library and return to my room. Eliza will surely be waiting for me and today I will surprise her and come to her so that she doesn't have to try and find me in this huge house that has more rooms than I can even imagine. At this point I will do anything to chase these absurd thoughts from my mind.

CHAPTER EIGHT

September 10, 1888

At dinner, Jax is in a better frame of mind and acts as if his earlier mood swing never happened. He makes no mention of Annie Chapman's murder, his reaction to the story, or where he has been the last three days. My curiosity is killing me, and I know that if I don't ask him where he has been, paranoia will consume me. However, I decide to wait until later to ask him.

As usual, after dinner we retire to the private sitting room. I figure that now is as good as time as any to ask, so I take a few minutes to build up the courage and then say, "Jax, may I ask you something?" He's hardly spoken to me since he returned, but I did get several soft caresses and smiles through dinner. I really don't know why I am afraid to ask him such a thing, but if this were Joe and I asked he'd tell me that it was none of my business and that I wasn't his keeper.

"Of course, my dear," he replies sweetly.

"Well, I've been wondering where you went. I know you said that something came up, but you never said what it was."

He looks over at me curiously and then says, "Oh my dear, you were worried about me, weren't you?" I nod. "My precious, precious Marie. I am sorry for making you worry about me. I should have told you the minute I returned home." He comes over and sits next to me. Taking my hand and bringing it to his lips, he says, "I'm not used to sharing my life with someone and sometimes I forget that we are together. Forgive me?"

"Yes, of course," I reply. *Now tell me where you were,* I think to myself.

He is silent for several minutes and I begin to think that his sweetness and apology was just a ruse so that he wouldn't have to answer my question, but then to my surprise he takes a deep breath and begins to speak. "What I am about to tell you, Marie, is very personal. Even my staff does not know, except for Rothschild, but they also know not to question me. Normally I would not share this with anyone, but I see the worry and concern in your eyes and I never want you to feel insecure when you are with me. I believe we have found a mutual connection, you and me, and I would hate for something like this to ruin that."

He sighs and then continues, "My sister, Victoria, is an opium addict. Many times, I am summoned to collect her or find her in the middle of the night."

"Collect her?" I ask.

"Yes, she gets herself in situations that, when under the influence, she cannot get out of. I have people watching her and although they are usually more than capable of dealing with her themselves, she only responds to me when she is in such a state."

"Where do you have to go?"

"Whitechapel," he replies.

I gasp. "That's why you were in Whitechapel the night we met! That's why you were in a hurry in the alley coming from Buck's Row." I pause and ask, "Why were you gone for three days?"

He looks down and then back at me. "Victoria refuses to come here, so I stay with her until she comes down from the high. Normally it's only a day, sometimes maybe two, but this time was a bad one and I was needed a little longer."

Relief washes over me; I know now that Jax is not the murderer in Whitechapel as I had so unjustly suspected. He has completely explained his reason for being there then and his whereabouts over the last several days. "Oh Jax, I'm so sorry," I say.

He waves his hand dismissively. "Don't be. She is the one you should feel sorry for. I do what I can for her. She does not want help so things will never change. I guess in a way I'm nothing short of the devil himself because I enable her. But I made a vow to her that I would always be there to take care of her. And I won't break it."

"I am witness to that. You drop whatever you are doing to be there for her. I wish I had a brother that cared about me like that. You're a good man, Jax," I say lovingly.

"Yes, but I tell you sometimes I think we both would be better off if I just wash my hands of her. Maybe she would sink so low that she wouldn't have a choice but to come to me for help. Then again, maybe she would just give up and eventually kill herself." He runs his hands through his hair in frustration. Shaking his head, he says, "I don't know, Marie, I really don't know."

"May I ask another question?" I ask.

"You can ask me anything. You know more about me than most people. To you, I'm an open book."

"Why were you so angered when you read about the second murder victim in Whitechapel today?" I know I should have just kept my mouth shut about this, but my subconscious was gnawing at me and I just had to know.

"These murders that have been happening in Whitechapel, not just Mary Ann Nichols and Annie Chapman, but all the ones before this ... they terrify me. My biggest fear is that I'm going to read about Victoria next." He shakes his head and then continues, "You've known me long enough to know that I'm always in control. Knowing that there is something out there that could have such a huge impact on my life that I have no control over angers me beyond reason. I stormed out of the library today because the last thing I wanted to do was unleash that anger on you."

"What can I do to help?" I ask. I feel so helpless; seeing him so torn and frustrated makes my heart ache.

A sinister smile spreads across his face. "Do you really want to help?" he asks.

The look on his face leaves me breathless. I know exactly where he is going with this and the anticipation excites me. "Yes," I whisper.

Getting up from the settee, he reaches for my hand and says, "That's my girl." I take his hand and rise. I am eager to find out what this beautiful man has in store for me tonight. I am going to show him just how much I missed him.

Once in the bedroom, Jax removes my nightdress, gown, and undergarments and lays me on the bed. I'm completely naked and bare to him. My thoughts of pleasuring him tonight fall to the wayside as he makes his intentions perfectly clear.

After removing his clothes, he climbs onto the bed. His arm snakes around my waist as he pulls me close. With featherlike touches, his hands graze along my breasts, down to my stomach, and eventually one hand falls between my legs. My legs fall open to him, my arousal already beginning to heighten at his touch. He inserts his fingers, two I think, inside me and my head falls back at the pleasure he is giving me. *Yes, I did miss him.*

I have had a lot of sex in my day, but it's never been something I've wanted, not even with my husband. I would give my body to anyone for rent money and food. It always was a means for survival. But with Jax, I can't seem to get enough of his touch. My body craves him and I find myself with more desire than I ever imagined. I could do this every night and never tire of the incredible pleasure he affords me. His thumb begins to massage my clit while the other two fingers are still inside me. *Oh God. I'm so close!* But to my surprise, just as I am about to find my release he stops. *No!*

"Jax, please," I beg.

He chuckles low in this throat as he clasps my hips and turns me over. "You'll learn. When I am done with you, Marie, I'll have taken you to the peak of the mountain, teetering on the edge, but never letting you fall until your frustration overtakes you and you are begging me to let you come."

"Jax, please, I am begging you now," I try to plead with him.

"Oh baby, you don't know what it means to beg. Let me show you." I realize that this is his way of regaining control. He needs this.

His hands graze up and down my spine administering the lightest of touches. My skin prickles with pleasure and I begin to squirm. I need him *there*. I think he heard my silent plea as he nudges my legs apart. Grasping my hips again, he pulls me up onto my hands and knees. I prepare for him to take me this way, but instead of doing what I expect, he places his fingers deeps inside and pumps, hitting that one spot inside of me that drives me insane. I'm reaching that peak again and just as I'm ready to come, he does it again. *Jax, NO!*

The pressure that I feel is unlike anything I have ever felt before. I'm desperate, wanton, and on the verge of insanity; all I can think about is coming. I feel as if he is worshiping me and punishing me all at the same time. *Remember, Marie, he needs this.*

"Jax!" I cry. He chuckles again and flips me over again onto my back. My pelvis is squirming for any type of friction.

I can't take it anymore and I reach down to pleasure myself, giving me my own release, but he knocks my hand away and holds both hands together. His grip on my wrists is like a steel cuff. He kneels between my legs, holding my wrists against my belly as he bends and starts dropping kisses against my inner thigh. First the right and then the left, stopping just inches from my throbbing pussy. *Insanity.* He is teasing me beyond my comprehension. I close my eyes and try to calm the fire that is raging inside of me. And then his hot breath hits my clit as his tongue plunges inside of me. *Oh God. Oh God, I'm coming.*

He's devouring me and lapping at the arousal he has created. Again, he pulls out and a tortured cry escapes my lips. His mouth hovers over me as he looks at me and says, "I told you that you would beg."

"Jax, I am begging. Please don't stop. I'll do anything," I cry in desperation.

This time, he does what I ask and dips down to tongue at my clit. I know I am going to die, I can feel it. The pressure is too much and it keeps building and building. *I'm so close ... please, Jax, give this to me.* My body begins to tense and I find that I am terrified that he will stop. He wants me to beg? Well, that's what he will get.

"Oh God, Jax, I'm begging you, please don't stop."

"Yes!"

The pressure continues building until it has nowhere to go and explodes in the most mind-numbing orgasm I have ever experienced. My breathing is heavy and I am utterly spent. Kissing up my body, he finally finds my mouth and kisses me. "Goodnight, beautiful Marie. Sweet dreams," he whispers.

He moves to lie next to me, pulling me close. As I lay there, completely sated, I realize I never took care of him. "What about you?"

"Tonight, my pet, was all for you. Now sleep." He kisses behind my ear. Too tired to argue, I let sleep take over my body.

CHAPTER NINE

September 22, 2018

Over the course of the last two weeks, Jax and I fell into a comfortable domestic pattern. We dine together every night. After dinner we spend an hour or so relaxing in his personal sitting room, Jax always reading the paper and me reading a book from his library. Then we retire to his bedchamber and fuck until the wee hours of the morning. I always wake alone and am left to spend my days on my own until dinner. I have been with him now for almost a month and every day I fall deeper and deeper in love.

Today, I am feeling exceptionally emotional. The reality of this weighs on me heavily; I am deeply in love with a man who has made it perfectly clear from day one that he will not fall in love with me. I believe his words were, *'I will fuck you and that's all'*, or something like that. What do I do with that?

I've stopped spending my afternoons in Whitechapel. There's nothing there for me anymore. I've tried to see Joe on several occasions, but he's never home. Finally I realized it was a waste of time spending my days in Whitechapel, a place I no longer belong. I decided to make one last attempt to talk to him about all this and wrote him a letter. It was difficult to take pen to paper and say everything that I wanted, but it became easier once I'd started. The letter read:

Dearest Joe,

I am terribly sorry about how we left things the last time I spoke. I know you don't understand my reasoning and you think that I left solely for the money, but that is not the case. This was something that I felt compelled to do for many reasons. There are other things happening with me and I just wanted you to know that it is nothing against you personally. I care very deeply for you, Joe, and am very grateful for all that you have done for me. I love you. However, I am not in love with you. Perhaps that seems harsh and unfeeling, but I feel that I need to be completely honest with you. I hope that someday you will forgive me, as I value your friendship immensely.

If you would like to write back, I will leave you with this: #24 St. James Park. I strongly suggest a letter, as it would not be prudent for you to arrive in person.

Forgive me,
Marie

The letter was delivered three days ago and I have not heard a word since. I really don't expect to hear back from him and I truly don't blame him for washing his hands of me. I know by sending that letter I have completely dispossessed myself of a home. But I also know that I have given him closure and I need not worry about him anymore. I have no idea what my future holds for me, but Joe is a part of my past, not my future.

I know that I am not a nice person. I use people until I no longer need them. I've done some horrific things in my past. I've hurt people and left them broken in my wake. Perhaps that is what I did with Joe.

When I first came to London, I found employment in an upper-class brothel in the West End. There, I was treated like royalty, having my own carriage and some of the most beautiful dresses I have ever seen. Well, until I looked inside my wardrobe at Jax's home.

Anyway, I met a man that requested my services often. His requests became more and more frequent. One day he professed his love for me and asked me to move to Paris with him. I refused. He became angry and hurt, but I felt nothing. I used him and made him think that I cared for him because he paid me well. He showered me with gifts of jewels, clothes, and trinkets. I didn't care that I hurt him. I didn't care that his heart was breaking. I walked away and never looked back. That's how I ended up in Whitechapel. I couldn't risk seeing him again in the West End.

I have a few friends, but most people don't like me. Which is why I cannot fathom my good fortune in finding Jax. I constantly wonder what I did to deserve him. In my opinion, I don't deserve him. But finding Jax has given new meaning to my life. I'm experiencing what it is like to actually be in love. I thought I loved my husband. I thought he was my salvation from an arranged marriage, but the love I feel for Jax is so much deeper. I know now what it's like to be selfless and put another person's needs before my own. So, I vow that I will strive to be a better person. For him. He deserves so much more than me.

I shake my head. My emotions are all over the place. *Why do these thoughts consume me? I need to go out today. Perhaps reading all these melancholy stories that I get from Jax's library has affected my mood.* Getting up from the settee in Jax's library, I walk out into the hallway and begin searching for Rothschild. After finding him in the hall outside the dining room, I ask, "Rothschild, would you please ask Jasper to prepare the carriage? I shall like to go out today."

"Of course, Miss Marie. Give him about thirty minutes," he replies.

"Perfect, that will give me an opportunity to freshen up a bit." I turn toward the foyer and the stairs and then turn back and say, "Thank you, Rothschild."

"My pleasure, miss."

Thirty minutes later I step out the front door and see Jasper waiting, as always, next to the carriage. When I approach, he takes my outstretched hand and guides me into the carriage. "Whitechapel, Miss Marie?"

"No," I reply. "I'd like to go to the marketplace, if you please."

"Of course, Miss Marie." He pauses and then adds, "Any place in particular?"

"Yes. The millinery, please."

I have not spent any of the money that Jax has given me over the last several weeks and am currently the proud owner of six pounds. I have been saving this money to ensure that I have a warm and dry place to sleep when this is all over, but today, I am buying myself a new hat. I haven't bought something frivolous and new for myself in years. Now that I have the means to do so, nothing is going to stand in my way.

As the carriage pushes on toward my shopping adventure, I take in the beautiful sights that surround me. This part of London is so different from the East End that I find it hard to believe that we are only a few miles apart.

The grandeur of this part of town is intoxicating, with the many ladies and their gentlemen strolling the streets and hustling about. The sun shines brightly on the buildings as we cruise down the theater district. As we travel down Piccadilly, I think, *Oh, how I would love to attend the theater. Perhaps I shall ask Jax if we could go some evening.* I chuckle to myself. *Who am I fooling?*

After stopping in front of The Top of Fashion, a shop that I would never dream of frequenting in a million years, Jasper comes around to the side and holds out his hand to escort me from the carriage.

"Shall I go in with you, miss?" he asks.

"No, Jasper, I shall be fine. Thank you." I turn toward the shop and then turn back to Jasper and add, "I won't be long."

He nods and I turn and proceed into the shop. The hats are beautiful and my fingers itch to try every one of them on. A woman approaches me and asks, "May I help you?"

At first I want to tell her no thank you, but then I decide that it might be fun to allow her to assist me in picking out something suitable. Suitable for what, I have no idea ... perhaps a hat for the theater? Yes, I think a hat for the theater.

"Yes, you may help me. I'm looking for a hat for the theater. Something quite fashionable and unique, if you please," I reply.

"Of course, allow me to show you our latest fashions," she says as she begins to walk to a counter that displays some of the prettiest hats I have ever seen. You would never see these hats in Whitechapel.

She goes through all the hats that she has on display and I discover that one stands out beyond all others. The hat is absolutely stunning; it has a stunted black top hat as the base and is adorned with a sparkly burgundy band. Black and burgundy feathers spring from the top, a black rose rests on the brim, and black tulle hangs from the back. As she places it on my head, she drapes the tulle around my right shoulder. I turn to look in the mirror and I simply fall in love with it.

"Oh, this is lovely," I say. "But I think that I will shop around." I hate to see the disappointment on her face, but I am sure that I do not have enough money to purchase it.

"I am so sorry, I really think this one is perfect for you," she replies.

"It is, but I don't want to make a hasty decision. Thank you for your time."

She nods and I turn to leave the shop. As I approach the carriage, Jasper asks, "Did you find anything you liked, Miss Marie?"

"I did!" I exclaim. "But I don't think I have enough money for it."

"What do you mean, you don't think you have enough money?" he asks.

"Well, I never asked how much it was. I was too embarrassed to ask the shopkeeper," I reply.

Before I can say another word, Jasper says, "Well, let's get you home then," and helps me in the carriage. Coming around to the window, he says, "If you will excuse me, miss, I shall be right back and then we can be on our way."

I watch him as he proceeds to enter the shop that I just exited. *What on earth is he doing?* I think for a moment and decide, *Perhaps he is buying a gift for his sweetheart. He has never talked about a female friend or companion, but that doesn't mean he doesn't have one.*

A few minutes later he returns with a hatbox. Opening the door to the carriage, he hands the box to me and says, "For you, miss."

"Uh, Jasper, I don't understand." I ask curiously, "Why would you buy me a hat?"

"I didn't," he replies. "The Master gave me strict instructions that if there was anything you wanted to purchase you were not to use your own money. He told me that whatever you wanted, I was to purchase it for you on his behalf."

"What? Why didn't I know about this?" I ask, stunned by the news.

"Well, miss, today was the first time you wanted to buy something. We've spent our days in Whitechapel and have never had the opportunity for you to shop."

Well, I never thought about that, but he is right. This was the first time that I have gone out to someplace other than Whitechapel. I think about what Jasper just told me and I wonder why Jax never informed me that if I wanted anything he would buy it. *Could he be testing me? But why? He knows that I entered into this agreement for the money. Well, at least in the beginning. He will never know that I stay for another reason.*

Looking down at the hatbox, I realize that it is just the thing to cheer me up.

"Jasper, have you ever been to the theater?" I'm not sure why I ask him this, but he really is the only person I have to converse with during the day and I have become quite fond of him.

"No, Miss Marie, I have not," he replies.

"Oh," I reply, disappointed. I was hoping that he would be able to tell me what it's like.

"Why do you ask?" he asks curiously.

"Oh, it's nothing, really," I reply, now embarrassed that I asked in the first place.

"Now Miss Marie, you can tell me. We're friends, are we not?"

"I guess," I reply shyly. I do think Jasper and I have become friends over the last several weeks. We have discussed many topics and engaged in many friendly debates on politics and authors.

"So, why did you ask me about the theater?"

"Well, I have never been and I thought maybe if you had been you could tell me what it's like."

"But what made you think about the theater? Was it our ride through Piccadilly?"

"Yes, partly, but I also thought that my new hat would be pretty to wear to the theater."

"Indeed it would, Miss Marie, indeed it would," he replies. When the silence settles between us, he adds, "Where to, miss?"

"The park, Jasper. I shall like to take a stroll in the park."

"St. James, miss?"

"Yes, please."

Jasper casually guides us through the park. I am in awe of all the ladies and gentlemen that are enjoying this beautiful fall afternoon. Many appear to not have a care in the world and I find myself wanting that life for myself. We arrive home around five; I have just enough time to dress for dinner. Jax should be home at any minute and I can't wait to show him my new hat.

What started out to be such a melancholy day has turned itself around and is getting much better by the minute.

When I come down the stairs for dinner, I find Jax waiting at the bottom. Holding his hand out, he says, "You look beautiful."

"Thank you," I reply as he escorts me into the dining room.

Once we are seated and the servers begin to serve our meal, Jax says, "I'm told that you went to the marketplace today."

Is there anything he doesn't miss? "I did," I say excitedly. When he doesn't respond, I add, "I found a lovely hat today. Jasper told me what you instructed him to do. Thank you, Jax. You've done so much for me; you really do not need to buy me things. But I am grateful and I can't thank you enough for everything."

He smiles. "Oh, my pet, there is no need to thank me. It pleases me to shower you with presents. Which reminds me, I have another present for you."

"You do?" I exclaim. I feel like a child on her birthday.

"I was also informed of something else today. Something I should have asked you about from the start, but neglected to."

"Oh?"

"I understand that you would like to attend the theater."

"I would," I say eagerly.

"Good, then we shall attend the theater. I shall get us tickets at the Adelphi in Covenant Garden. Would you like that?"

The day just keeps getting better and better. I can't believe that he is taking me to the theater on Monday. I know that my excitement is beaming across my face, but I just can't contain it. I rise impulsively from my seat to hug him and plant a kiss on his cheek. Realizing that this behavior isn't appropriate, I quickly return to my seat and sit down.

"My apologies," I say, my eyes downcast.

Jax begins to laugh. "Oh, my pet, don't ever apologize for showing affection. Your passion is infectious and I wouldn't want it any other way."

"But I was not acting very ladylike," I say demurely.

He grins. "If I had wanted a lady, I would have a lady." He adds quickly, "I mean no offense to you, my dear. When I refer to a lady, I'm talking about one who revels in her accomplishments and refinements, who boasts of her good breeding and lineage. No, I want a woman. You are a woman, an incredibly strong and passionate woman. Don't ever change what you are."

I've never seen Jax this lax with his compliments before. It's as if something has shifted between us. Something has definitely changed, but I cannot for the life of me figure out what it is. This man, he is such an enigma to me. One minute I think I have him figured out and next I am quickly stunned back into ignorance.

After dinner, we retire to the sitting room as usual. Jax peruses the paper while I pick up where I left off in my book. Today, I am reading Jane Austen's Pride and Prejudice. I love her dry humor and wit as well as her perceptions about London society. She makes me laugh with her satire.

Later, lying in bed listening to the soft gentle snores of the man next to me, I realize that I never showed him my new hat.

I've never seen her so happy. Shopping suits her. Her smile is infectious and only enhances her beauty.

CHAPTER TEN

September 24, 1888

Today we attend the Union Jack at the Adelphi Theater. Jax informed me last night before we retired for bed that we would be dining out before the performance. He told me that I should get as much rest as I could today so that I could fully enjoy the night he had planned for us both. He also instructed me to be ready by six.

So, like a good girl, I do as I am told. I take my breakfast in my room and remain in bed a bit longer than normal. My book is lying on the nightstand and so I begin to get lost in the world of the Bennets of Longbourn and the Darcys of Pemberley. After about a couple of hours I'm startled by a knock at the door. I realize I still haven't dressed for tonight and I assume it is Eliza to prepare my bath.

Putting on my dressing gown, I reply, "Come in." To my surprise, in walks Rothschild with a rather large box. "What is this?" I ask.

"For you, miss. It arrived just now. From the Master, I presume." He bows.

"Thank you, Rothschild."

"If I may, Miss Marie—are you well?" he asks.

"Oh yes, I am very well, thank you. I am just resting a little longer today than usual. The Master and I will out late this evening."

"Ah, yes, he did mention that this morning before he left. It slipped my mind." He pauses and then adds, "Well, if that will be all." He turns to leave.

"Actually, Rothschild, could you ask Eliza to come up, please?" I ask.

"Of course." When Rothschild leaves I scurry to the box on the bed. Opening it up, I see the most beautiful black and burgundy dress I have ever seen. *How did he know?* The dress matches my hat perfectly, as if they were meant to be worn together. I'm stunned. *Really, how did he know?* I ask myself again. I find it a bit unnerving that he knows so much. But I shrug it off when I look back at my new dress.

Eliza comes in not long after Rothschild leaves and we spend the rest of the day primping and coiffing me into perfection. Even I am surprised with the finished product. I stand before the mirror in awe of the woman before me. I've never imagined that I would be dressed so elegantly, about to attend a performance at the Adelphi Theater at Covenant Garden. *It doesn't get any better than this.*

As I make my way down the stairs at half past five, I am surprised to see that Jax is home. He is talking with Rothschild in the foyer below. He's already dressed for tonight in a dark tailcoat, burgundy vest, and white shirt. His dark hair is wavy and silky, the curls barely resting on his broad and masculine shoulders. He's breathtakingly handsome and I have to stop for a moment just to take him in.

When I proceed down the stairs, my gown rustles. As if on cue, both men turn their heads at the sound and the look of awe on their faces warms my heart. I smile and continue to descend down the stairs.

"We'll discuss this later," Jax says to Rothschild in a stern voice. Rothschild nods and turns to leave.

Jax stands at the bottom of the stairs and does nothing but stare at me as I approach. Taking my hand into his, he says, "You, my pet, are a vision." He pauses and then adds, "I am in awe of your beauty." He bends and kisses my hand. Tingles run up my arm and down my spine. All it takes is one feather-light kiss on my hand from this man and my body turns to mush.

I love you, I silently say to him. My words are silent for I know I will never utter them aloud to him. I will never put myself in a position of having my heart broken. *Isn't that what you have already done?* my subconscious admonishes me.

"Shall we?" he asks. "We are a bit early for dinner, but I thought we could ride through the park prior to dinner."

"That would be lovely. Thank you."

Once we are settled in the carriage, I realize that this is not the same carriage that has been at my disposal, nor is Jasper the driver. This is the same carriage that we used when Jax took me to his home that first night.

"Where is Jasper?" I ask.

"Jasper is your driver, Marie. Carlton is my driver," he replies.

"But this carriage is different," I say.

"Yes, it is. I have a few carriages, but this is the one I use most frequently. Actually, I prefer it."

"Oh, I see."

As we proceed, I realize we are not heading toward St. James Park. *We must be going to a different park,* I think curiously. I become excited when the driver turns into Hyde Park.

"Oh Jax, this is wonderful!" I exclaim.

"Have you ever been?" he asks.

Fidgeting like a child, I reply, "No, never. I've always wanted to, but was never presented with the opportunity."

"Good, then I have done my job. If you haven't figured out by now, Marie, my goal is to give you everything you always wanted but don't have. I want you to experience things like you have never experienced them before. I want to show you the world during our time together."

And how long will that be? I ask myself, desperately wanting him to give me the answer. I look at him curiously. He's never said anything like this before and I am a bit perplexed by what he says. "Jax ..." I pause, unsure of my next words. Cautiously, I continue,

"What are you saying?" My heart is racing at the prospect of what he just said. *Is he making this permanent?*

"Nothing really, I just want you to enjoy the time you have with me. That's all."

Those two simple sentences totally shatter all my hopes. For a minute, he was so different; it seemed like he was professing something like love. I know it. I could feel it in his words and his tone. But then he caught himself and completely changed. *But why?*

Nothing more is said on the subject. Trying to forget the pain in my heart, I look out the window of the carriage and admire the park. I find the spectacle of London society amusing and wonderful all at the same time. Never in all my days have I seen such a display of beauty and elegance in one place.

As the carriage rolls through, we come to an intersection in the roadway. A gentleman dressed in a royal guard's uniform motions for us to stop and move over to the side. As I look around, I see other carriages and pedestrians directed to do the same. The crossing road is left unencumbered by any traffic.

"What is happening, Jax?" I ask curiously.

"We shall see, my pet. Be patient," he replies, giving me nothing else.

And then I see it. Casually rolling down the roadway is a great carriage with outriders and several gentlemen riding alongside. The landau holds four passengers and is pulled by four very majestic horses. As it rides by, I see the royal coat of arms on the door. "Is that ..." I am too shocked to continue; I sit there in disbelief as I watch the carriage roll by.

"Yes, my dear. That's Queen Victoria," he replies knowingly. He adds, "You know, it is rumored that she rarely spends time in London, let alone goes out. Perhaps she knew you would be here today to see her and so she made the effort," he says teasingly.

"Oh how you tease me!" I admonish him.

"Look," he says.

I look back over to where the Queen just passed by and see that she is followed by another carriage. The people milling around watching it pass by cheer excitedly. I see that there is a woman in the carriage and I am pretty sure I know who it is. "Princess Alexandra?" I ask Jax.

He nods. "You see how popular she is with the people. England loves her," he says fondly; I can see he feels the same way.

After the princess passes, many landaus, barouches, and victorias follow. It's like a fairy tale. *Who am I kidding? My whole life has turned into a fairy tale ever since Jackson Kent stepped into my life.*

"Happy?" he asks with a smile.

"Oh yes, Jax, thank you!" I reply. He takes his walking stick and taps the roof of the carriage. "Carlton, to the Adelphi please."

The carriage turns toward the way we arrived; we are now off to the theater. *Could this night get any better? I can't believe that I saw the Queen and Princess!*

We have a lovely dinner at the plaza, even though the entire time I feel out of place. I feel that everyone is staring at me and can tell where I am from. Several times throughout dinner, I not only get the feeling that everyone in the restaurant can see right through me, but that there is something sinister in the room. This isn't a feeling of being out of place, this is a feeling of being watched. I would even go as far as to say a feeling of being stalked. It causes the hair on the back of my neck to rise; my skin prickles and I shudder at the thought.

"Marie, are you unwell?" Jax asks, concerned.

I shake my head. "No, no, I am wonderful. Sorry, I just had an odd feeling of being watched," I reply.

"Oh, my dear, you must get used to that. You are beautiful and your gown and hat are stunning on you. Of course people will watch you," he replies.

I do not reply and we continue to finish our dinner. When we are done, we depart the plaza and proceed to the theater.

Several minutes later we pull up in front of the theater. If I thought the array of London society in the park was a bit of a spectacle, what appears before me is much worse. There are so many people gathered outside the theater dressed in the most beautiful clothes I have ever seen.

I quickly realize that this is a world I could never belong in. Everything about this—the theaters, the parks, and even Jax—it's all temporary. Saddened by this thought, coupled with Jax's indifference earlier in expressing his feeling for me or lack thereof, I want nothing more than to return to Whitechapel and my dim and boring poverty-stricken life.

Jax helps me from the carriage and escorts me to the door of the theater. Several people acknowledge him and he stops to converse on many occasions. I swear everyone here knows him. He is polite to others, but he never introduces me or acknowledges me except for his arm intertwined with my own. It is obvious we are together, but nobody asks about me or acknowledges me either. It's as if I don't exist. Sadness overwhelms me as we move toward the staircase outside the main hall.

After climbing up two flights, we are escorted to our seats in a private box. *He has a private box? Who is this man who knows everyone, has wealth beyond anything I could imagine, and makes love like a god?* I pause and think sadly, *And who will toss me back to the wretched world from which I came.*

I admonish myself, *No! I will not let my melancholy and depressing mood ruin this night for me! I will not!*

Perking back up, I look up at Jax. For a moment I just stare at him. He's so handsome, his features strong and masculine. His dark hair is wavy and silky and his gray eyes have a softness to them that makes me melt. He turns toward me when he realizes that I am staring and says, "What is it?"

"I just wanted you to know that I am having a wonderful time tonight. Thank you."

"Oh my pet, the night has just begun. I have many surprises in store for you tonight." He pauses and then adds, "Here," handing me the playbill for tonight's performance.

Looking at the playbill, I finally learn what the play is about. The front of the playbill reads:

> *The Union Jack by Henry Pettitt and Sydney Grundy.*
> *Jack Medway (a sailor) played by William Terriss and*
> *Ethel Arden by Jessie Millward.*
> *Rose cottage designed by William Perkins.*

I notice a note on the playbill that reads:

> *Theatre lighted entirely by electricity by the Edison and Swan United Electric Company.*

Oh my! Astonished, I quickly look around the theater. Electricity! No gaslights or flames. Real electricity! I hadn't even noticed it. Tugging on Jax's arm, I say, "Jax, look at this." I show him the note on the playbill.

He nods. "Yes, my dear. Electricity. Isn't it wonderful? I hope to have the house wired in the near future."

"It's amazing. I never thought I would ever see such a thing."

"Yes, another surprise." He chuckles. For a brief moment he almost sounds sinister.

Chills run down my spine at the tone in his voice. I turn to face him and his eyes are dark and penetrating. *Does he have other surprises planned?* I wonder. The chills turn to anticipation as I think about what he could have planned for me later.

The play comprises four acts. After each act, the house lights go on and everyone gets up and convenes in the lobby. Ten minutes later, a young man walks through the lobby with a bell shouting, "Five minutes!" and everyone begins to move back toward their seats. The whole process floors me. I have never seen so much pomp and circumstance in all my days, even in my younger days when I was considered a lady back in Ireland. But we Irish are of a different breed. We are more heart and soul than pomp and circumstance.

When the play is over, everyone stands outside waiting for their carriages to be brought forth. Ours is one of the first to arrive and Jax quickly escorts me in and Carlton drives off.

"Did you enjoy the play?" he asks.

"I did. Thank you so much for tonight," I reply.

"All this was for you, my pet—the park, the Queen, the play. All for you," he says and again I see that soft caring side that wants to tell me he loves me. But this time, I know better than to hope and I don't even respond to his words. I just let them lie between us, sucking up all the air as the carriage becomes stifling.

We remain silent as Carlton navigates the short distance back to Jax's home. Once at the house, Jax helps me from the carriage and we walk toward the door. When we get to the door, he leans down and whispers in my ear. "I have a few things to attend to before I retire for the night." I'm about to reply when he kisses the spot behind my ear and hovers there and says, "I expect you naked and in my bed by the time I am through." All the breath leaves my body as I nod. When we enter the house, he warns, "I won't be long."

Her beauty consumes me.

Does she know how much I love her?

CHAPTER ELEVEN

Moving as quickly as I can without making a spectacle of myself, I hurry up the stairs. Eliza is in my room waiting for me and she helps me undress. Once I am situated in my nightclothes, I dismiss Eliza and proceed to Jax's bedchamber.

He's not there and I breathe a sigh of relief. The last thing I want to do is disappoint him by not being ready when he arrives. I quickly remove my nightdress and undergarments. Completely naked, I slip into bed.

As I lie there, I think about what a wonderful night it has been. The park, the Queen, the theater ... everything was out of a dream for me. But the anticipation of what's to come is making me antsy. *Where is he? What is taking him so long?*

Perhaps if I try to sleep while I wait, the wait won't seem so long. Turning on my side, facing away from Jax's side of the bed, I close my eyes and try to find sleep.

I'm awoken by a single finger slowly tracing down the center of my spine. Jax's hot breath on my neck sends shivers through my body. I don't want to move or distract him from the glorious pleasure that he is giving me. I stay completely still, basking in the sensations he awakens all over my body. I sigh with a slight moan, indicating to him that I am awake and am perfectly content.

"I've awakened you," he says.

"Umhmmm," I mumble lazily. His touch is leaving a trail of goosebumps down my spine, settling at the base of my tailbone. When his hand reaches the indentation of my lower back my body involuntarily reacts and my bottom rises, begging for his touch. My breath hitches as his hand moves down to caress my bottom. My body comes alive and suddenly I am on fire with an urgency that only he can control.

His hand reaches down my behind and in between my legs. He inspects my pussy with his finger and moans, "My pet, you are already wet for me. I am pleased."

As his fingers explore my pussy, I lose all control of my body and I begin to fuck his fingers. Pleasure consumes my entire body as his two fingers reach that spot that drives me to the edge of insanity. *Oh yes!* Just when I am about to detonate on his hand, he stops. *No! Oh no, not again!*

"Jax," I moan. "Please," I beg, desperate for the friction.

Whispering in my ear, he says, "Lie on your back."

Slowly, I turn my body over, doing as he instructed. I am now completely exposed to him. The covers on the bed have long been pushed away. Taking the same finger he used to caress my back, he runs it down the center of my body, stopping just before reaching the patch of blonde curls between my legs. I grunt in frustration. He's teasing and toying with me.

As his fingers slowly travel across my body, he circles my breasts but barely grazes over my nipples. I look up at him in awe of the man who is so intent on providing me pleasure. The look in his eyes is dark, sultry and almost sinister. I wonder what he's thinking; I quickly conclude that I don't want to know. I'm already lost to this man and I fear that if I get inside his head I will get sucked in deeper in an abyss of darkness that I won't be able to escape.

"Jax, please." His ministrations continue and I am filled with pent-up sensations that need to be released. I need him. I need his cock.

Before I know what is happening, the bed dips and I realize that he is getting up off the bed. *No!* Walking over to my side of the bed, he begins to remove his clothes. I look away out of politeness, but his words bring my eyes back to him.

"Watch me, Marie."

So I do. He takes his time and I swear he is doing this to antagonize me more than he already has. Once every article of clothing has been removed from his body, I look at the Adonis before me. He's beautiful. Taking in his broad chest, chiseled abs and a very sexy strand of dark hair that leads to his pubic area, my breath hitches. Once I work my eyes down to his cock I see that he is hard, swollen and pulsing. There is a spot of dampness on the tip and I suddenly have the urge to lick it clean. To know that I have done this to him is intoxicating.

He saunters over to the bed and bends down to kiss me. My hands immediately reach for his cock but he grabs them both with one hand and holds them tight while his tongue invades my mouth. I want to touch him. I need to touch him. But at the same time, not being able to touch him and being restrained by his firm grasp heightens the sensation of his lips on mine. My body squirms.

Once he releases my hands, I reach for him and take hold of his cock. I am convinced that it gives me more pleasure than him as I stroke him, feeling him grow and harden more from my touch. My thumb grazes the head and I see that drop of wetness that I witnessed earlier is still there; I now need to take him in my mouth. But as I move to get closer to him, rising from the bed, he pushes me back down.

"Do you want me inside you?" he asks.

"Yes," I breathe.

He crawls up on the bed and I am disappointed briefly when he positions himself over my pussy instead of moving up my body to my mouth. My disappointment quickly fades once his length is fully sheathed inside me. He fills me completely and stays that way, allowing me to get accustomed to his size. Once I begin to move my hips his movement resumes. He moves in and out of me so slowly; I can feel the difference in his mood from all the other times before. This is not fucking. This is passion and love; he is savoring every moment inside of me. I feel every inch of him and the pressure builds with each movement he makes.

He grabs both of my hands in one of his and holds them above my head. The urge to touch him increases now that I can't, but the power of him holding me like this turns me on even more. I arch my back into him, feeling everything he has to give.

He leans down and kisses me slowly and passionately as he lets out a moan that makes my insides heat. I'm on fire. The emotions that I am feeling now are unlike anything I have experienced before. The love that I feel for this man is overflowing and everything in me wants to tell him, wants him to know how I feel about him. And before I can consciously have a rational thought, I blurt out, "Jax, I love you!"

He stills, his cock inside of me and his hands restraining mine. He says nothing, but stares into my eyes. I am so torn by his sudden silent acknowledgement of my words that instead of keeping my mouth shut and waiting for some type of response from him, I repeat, "Jax, I love you." And then I begin to babble, "I know this was not part of our agreement, but I just couldn't...."

"Stop!" he bellows. Before I can say another word, he takes his hand from restraining mine and brings it to my throat. After gingerly laying his hand across my throat, he begins to move inside me again. But this time it's not slow and sensual. This time it is rough and demanding. The harder he thrusts, the harder his hand squeezes at my throat.

I can't breathe! I try to struggle to get free, but his grip is too strong. I claw at him, but I can't loosen the vice that surrounds my throat. It is like he is suddenly possessed by some type of dark demon. I realize that there is nothing I do can get through to him and make him stop. *I'm going to die.* Panic begins to take control of me as he continues to thrust inside of me. My vision begins to blur and I can feel myself losing consciousness. *Holy fuck, he's going to kill me!*

Oh my God, I'm dying! The pressure inside builds and my vision is almost gone. What seems like an eternity of teetering at death's door is literally only a few seconds when my body climaxes in a rush that obliterates me to the core. He releases my neck as I suck in a rush of air, gasping for life, while at the same time riding on a wave of the best orgasm I have ever had. *Holy fuck!*

The orgasm that takes over my body is mind blowing and earth shattering all at the same time. Every part of my body spasms with pleasure so intense I feel as if I am going to combust into nothingness, while still hungrily trying to take in as much air as I can into my lungs. He's still pumping into me, hard and persistent. With a loud growl he reaches his climax and totally fills me with his seed. When he comes down from his orgasm, he collapses on top of me, his hand still resting at my throat. *Oh my!*

My head is racing full of conflicting thoughts. *I was fucking terrified! But the rush was totally unbelievable. I feel revived and so alive!* He had me on the verge of death and brought me back to life. The force of his hand at my throat and his thrusts into my body was intoxicating and thrilling and terrifying all at the same time.

Now what?

I don't know what to say. I feel that something needs to be said, but I'm so afraid of setting him off again. But then a grin escapes my face and I think that perhaps I want to set him off again. I want him to do it again.

But instead I lie there unmoving underneath him. I wait for any type of words, reaction, or movement from him. After several agonizing minutes, he moves off of me and rolls on to his side of the bed, lying on his back. I'm still afraid to move until he reaches his arm over, inviting me to snuggle against him. Pulling me close, he kisses the top of my head and whispers, "I never wanted this. I should have stayed away. I told you that I would never love you. But fuck, I do, Marie. I love you."

The words I never imagined would fall from his lips land in a heap in the center of the room. I don't respond to them, instead I lie there quietly basking in the fact that yes, he does love me.

I love her!

Chapter Twelve

October 1, 1888

The last few days have passed in a blur of more sex than I could ever imagine. Something has changed between us, but I'm not sure whether it is because we have professed our love for each other, or something else. I hope that it is the former rather than the latter, but Jax is an enigma I find very hard to read most times.

And the sex, well ... nothing is consistent there. He has been kind and gentle at times and other times I see my life flash before my eyes. But neither one keeps me from loving him. I like his rough demanding side just as much as I like his gentle side.

I've been reading a new book from Jax's library: *The Strange Case of Dr. Jekyll and Mr. Hyde* by Robert Louis Stevenson. It's a horror story that was published just a couple of years ago. That's not usually my thing, but after living with Jax I can relate to this type of story better than I thought I would.

Basically, the book is about Henry Jekyll and the evil Mr. Hyde. A magic serum transforms Jekyll into Hyde in order for him to indulge in the darker side of his character. But over time, Jekyll allows the dark side to consume him and he finds that he is slowly becoming Hyde. It is a story that examines the multiplicity in a man and the tragic consequences that can occur when he allows the dark to control him.

The more I read, the more I can compare the struggle that this character endures with Jax. He definitely has a dark side. But I don't know if I am too blind to be scared of it or just too dumb to run away from it.

I brush off these confusing feelings and proceed to break my fast. Jax never returned home last evening, but since he told me about his sister, Victoria, I didn't worry. Hopefully he will return tonight.

Sitting at the table, I see that Rothschild has left *The London Times* for me. There, staring me blatantly in the face, is this morning's headline:

MORE MURDERS IN THE EAST END

Will this madness ever end? I ask myself. As I continue to read I am horrified to find out that in the early hours of yesterday morning, two more horrible murders were committed in the East End of London. The victims in both cases were believed to belong to the same unfortunate class as Mary Ann Nichols and Annie Chapman, the same class as me.

The article continues, stating that the scenes of the murders are within a quarter of an hour's walk of each other. The earlier was committed in a yard in Berner Street off Commercial road and the second in Mitre-Square, Aldgate. The first body, a Miss Elizabeth Stride, was found in a gateway leading to a factory, only having her throat cut. It says that they are sure that his intention was to mutilate the victim but it appeared that he had been interrupted. *Oh my God! Liz!*

Liz was my friend. We both worked for Madame Grace. I can't believe that she is dead and murdered by a lunatic. I think back to the last time I saw Liz. Time has melded together for me since I have been at St. James Park; at first I have trouble remembering. But then it hits me. I saw her the night after I ran into Jax in the alley. Liz and I were having a drink in the Ten Bells when Jax came in and literally swept me away.

It could have been me!

The reality of my thoughts consumes me. Liz and I always spent a lot of time together when we weren't working. I could have been with her and he could have killed us both. *Oh dear Lord! Jax has saved me from all of that.*

I cannot put the paper down and I continue to read:

> *The murder in Mitre Square shows that the assassin appears to be free from any fear of interruption. The constable's beat is patrolled in between fifteen and twenty minutes, and it is believed that the murderer and his victim arrived inside this interval. The deceased, Catherine Eddowes, was found lying on her back. Her throat was terribly cut with a large gash across her face from the nose to the right angle of her cheek. Part of her right ear had been severed.*

The article continues to state that there were other indescribable mutilations, including the lower part of the woman's body. They believe that the murderer possessed some type of anatomical skill. *Oh Lord, this cannot be happening. It must be the same person. But why?*

The question and the murders plague me. I try to do anything to erase these horrible thoughts from my mind, but nothing seems to work.

The last thing I read in the article is that the Whitechapel Vigilance Committee addressed a petition to the Queen praying that, in the interest of the public at large, she would direct an immediate offer of a large reward for the capture of the murderer. It was denied.

I put the paper down and rise from the table. The server standing behind me steps aside as I turn and rush out of the room. *I need air. I need to escape.* Running through the foyer, I practically bump into Rothschild.

He says, "Miss, are you alright?"

"I need to go out. Can you please ask Jasper to prepare the carriage, immediately?" I know I'm being abrupt with him, I know that I should have explained myself, but I just can't. I am feeling smothered, like something has taken hold of my heart and is trying to rip it out. *Two more murders. One so close, it could have been me. Mutilated bodies. It's too much.*

I wish Jax was here!
Why isn't Jax here?
He should be here.
Remember, he didn't come home last night.
Remember, Marie, remember!

My subconscious is shouting at me to remember. "What do you want me to remember?" I shout at nobody.

And then a chill runs down my spine. The pit of my stomach becomes empty and hollow and the hairs on the back of my neck begin to prickle.

The nightmare is forcing itself to the surface. I use all my strength to push it away, to hide it in the depths of my mind. But it's too strong. It's here, on the surface of my brain, screaming to come out ... and I'm devastated by it.

"No!" I shout. *He wouldn't! He couldn't!*

My heart drops to the floor as the cold hard truth slaps me in the face.

Jax was running in the alleyway from Bucks Row when Mary Ann Nichols was murdered!

Jax was out all night when Annie Chapman was murdered!

Jax met Liz!

The thoughts flood my brain and I want nothing more than to scream them away.

I won't go there! I won't betray my trust in him! I love him.

As I am being escorted into the carriage, the cool autumn breeze wafting over my face, a final thought enters my mind.

What a strange emotion love is. It can consume you beyond all reason and it can tear you up inside, making your heart bleed.

But now I've let the heinous acts in Whitechapel imbed themselves into the back of mind.

I can't help but question the man that I love and thought I knew so well.

Could he?

Would he?

An eerie calm comes over me as I ask Jasper to take me to Whitechapel.

Chapter Thirteen

It's been a couple of weeks since I've been back to Whitechapel. As Jasper moves us through the streets, I take in my surroundings and realize that this is my home. And as much as I don't want to admit it, it's my home because it's away from Jax. Right now being away from Jax is exactly what I need. I need to think, to put the pieces together and find out one way or another if he is the sadistic murderer of Whitechapel.

Just the thought of being in such proximity to such an animal makes my skin crawl. We were intimate. He professed his love and then murdered innocent women. But then my thoughts change and I remember how he made me feel. He was so kind to me, so passionate and sensual. He's been more than a companion; he's someone that I can see myself spending the rest of my life with. He's kind to me and doesn't treat me like a whore. To him, I'm a lady. How could he be a killer?

But how can I explain the evidence that has reared its ugly head and is pointing a finger directly at him? *Could it really be a coincidence? Am I being ridiculous?*

TALK TO HIM, MARIE! my subconscious screams at me. I do need to talk to him, but right now I am so rattled that for the first time, I'm afraid of him. I'm afraid to be in the same house as him. I'm even more afraid to be alone with him.

I've been so deep in thought that I didn't realize that we have arrived in Spitalfields. Jasper opens the carriage door and says, "Miss Marie, you didn't say where you wanted to go in Whitechapel—I assume here is your wish. If I'm wrong, I can take you wherever you want to go." I look beyond Jasper and see the old building that up until a month ago I called home.

Home. Maybe this is where I need to be. I really didn't think beyond having Jasper take me here, but perhaps this is the answer. This is where I can clear my head. *Is this still my home? Would Joe allow me to return? I really have no other place to go.*

And then I realize I have money. I have thirty crowns, one for each night I have spent with Jax. Suddenly I feel sick as I realize it was never anything but a business arrangement. Sure, we professed our love for each other, but although I truly had feelings for Jax, it was all business from him. He even warned me that he wouldn't fall in love. *Then why did he say it?*

Oh, bloody hell. If I don't stop these questions that plague my mind I will go crazy and that won't do me any good. I've survived on the streets of this district for years and I will continue to survive. The money I've earned over the last month will help to get me back on my feet again, but I know it won't last forever. I know that I will blow most of it, I know myself too well. It's not what I want to do, but I'll do it just the same. That's how I operate.

"Jasper, I will be staying in Whitechapel indefinitely. If you would, please return to St. James Park and inform your Master that our agreement has come to an end."

"But Miss Marie, he won't be pleased. He'll be angry with both of us if I don't return with you this evening," Jasper replies.

"I'm sorry, Jasper, truly I am. But there are things I need to figure out before I return. Assure the Master that I will return in a day or two, but right now I need to put some distance between us. Tell him that when I do return I won't be staying, but that we will need to talk."

"If you are upset about him not coming home last night, it can't be helped. I'm not supposed to know, but his sister ..."

I can't let him finish. I don't want to hear it. "I know all about his sister and no, that is not why I'm leaving. Just ... please, Jasper. I need to do this."

"But miss, I could lose my position," he says with desperation on his face. I don't want him to lose his job, but I have to do this.

With defeat in his eyes, he reaches his hand out to assist me from the carriage. "Forgive me for saying so, Miss Marie, but I shall miss you."

I reach up and touch the side of his face. He is a sweet man and I hate to see him so sad. "I will return, Jasper. If not for anything but to say goodbye. I shall see you soon." He nods and turns back toward the carriage.

As I watch Jasper drive away, a sense of panic washes over me. *What have I done? Did I just throw away everything that was good in my life?* The voices in my head begin to scream, *You're a fool! He's a murderer! A killer!* As much as I don't want to believe what my head is saying, my heart tries to intervene. *He loves you!* But to no avail, I reach my hands up to my ears, trying to drown out all the noise in my head and stand strong with my decision. Turning, I walk over toward my old home. Perhaps that might be the best place to start. Then I shake my head. No, I need to go somewhere fresh. Someplace where I can put my mind into a fresh attitude.

Leaving Miller's Court, I head down Commercial Street toward Whitechapel Road. Upon reaching the cross street of Wentworth I decide that I will pop into the Princess Alice Pub. The pub is on the eastern side of Commercial Street at the southern corner. I always loved this place. It is named after Queen Victoria's third child, Princess Alice Maud Mary, Duchess of Saxony. Arthur Ferrar is the current owner and landlord. Perhaps he has rooms to let for an old friend for a night or two.

As I walk through the door, a wave of familiarity washes over me. Here, I can be myself. Here, I don't have to be a lady. *Gawd! That sounds awful.* I walk up to the bar and take a seat on one of the vacant stools.

"Wet your whistle, Marie?" Harry the barman asks.

"Whiskey, please," I reply.

"Can't do any favors, Marie," he states authoritatively.

"I know, I know. I have money." I sigh and then add, "Last month was a good month." *Good month my ass. Last month was a dream and today, I single-handedly threw it all away. For what? Because I'm afraid to talk to the man that changed my life for the better ... the man I'm in love with. Damn you, Marie!*

"That'll be a pence," Harry says as he hands me the glass. I reach into my bag and lay the pence on the bar. He looks at me curiously and then takes the money. "I haven't seen you around much lately. Where ya been?" he asks.

"Oh, I was away for a while," I reply, trying very hard not to give anything away. My whereabouts are really none of his business anyway.

"You've missed all the excitement around here, then?" he asks.

"If you are talking about the murders, I've read about them in the papers. Ghastly business, Harry."

"It is. People are scared and business is hurting. Not just here, either; all over the district." He pauses briefly and then adds, "Have you read the morning edition of the *Daily News*?"

"No. I saw the *Times* earlier. What does the *Daily* say?"

"He's got a name, Marie," Harry replies as he reaches for the newspaper.

"What?" I reply, astonished.

"Yeah, calls himself Jack the Ripper." He hands me the paper and says, "Here, read this."

I take the paper from him and begin to read the article that he pointed at.

On 27 September 1888,

the Central News Office in London

received a letter,

signed by Jack the Ripper

Jack the Ripper?

Jack?

Jax?

Jackson Kent?

No!

I continue to read. The article continues to say that the letter they received is handwritten and the killer calls himself Jack the Ripper. I'm in shock as I look up at Harry and ask, "Do they know who he is?" Suddenly I'm afraid that Jax has been arrested. How sick is that?

"Naw, they still have no idea," he replies, shaking his head while he cleans one of the beer glasses left by another patron.

"Um, Harry, does Arthur have any rooms upstairs? Just for a night or two," I ask.

"What about Joe's place?" he asks.

"Harry, really. I just need a room. Got anything?" I say.

"Let me see what I can do." He puts the clean glass down under the bar and then says, "I'll be right back."

He comes back a few minutes later and says, "Marie, I got you a room. Four shillings a night, paid up front."

I reach in my bag again and pull out eight shillings and hand it over to him. "I'll be staying two nights. If I decide to stay longer, I'll let you know." Again, he looks at me in surprise and then takes the money. "Tell Arthur I said thank you." He nods.

"Come on, I'll show you to your room." He gestures toward the stairs and I follow behind.

Once in my room above the pub, I lie down on the bed. All the thoughts that I had hoped I would be rid of by being away are now crashing through my mind like waves in the ocean.

I really need to put this all in perspective.

Eventually, mental exhaustion takes over my body and I finally fall asleep.

You truly are a sleeping beauty.

Oh Marie, why did you leave me?

CHAPTER FOURTEEN

October 3, 1888

It has been two days since I left St. James Park and have been staying at the Princess Alice. I've spent my days wandering through the streets of Whitechapel, taking in my three favorite pubs and getting lost in the rubble that used to be my home. I have not taken any tricks. The thought of sleeping with another man repulses me.

Back at the Alice, I sit at the bar, my hand wrapped around my fourth, or fifth ... hell, I think it might be my sixth drink of the day and I am feeling it. But really, I don't care. I am done caring. My life is over. Jax took me in and treated me like a lady and I threw it all away and left. I never even gave him the chance to explain. I thought I could just walk right back into my old life, but I can't. There's no place for me here now. I can't return to my old profession and I have no other skills. I still have money left, but at the rate I am going and with all the alcohol I've consumed, it won't last much longer. That's the story of my life. Perhaps I will just go back to Ireland and wash my hands of England.

"Harry, I want anodder won plwese," I ask. It's getting really hard to talk. I sure as hell hope he understood me.

Harry brings over my drink and sits it down in front of me. I grab the drink I currently have and down it in one gulp and hand him the glass as I grab with my other hand the fresh drink he just brought me. "You staying here tonight, Marie?" he asks.

"Yesssss," I reply.

He holds his hand out and says, "Pay up, Marie."

I reach in my bag and hand him one pence for the drink and four shillings for the room. Tonight will be my last night here. I need to go back to St. James Park and talk to Jax. I doubt he will want to see me, but at least I can leave him with a clear conscience by thanking him and saying goodbye.

I finish my drink and look around the pub. I can tell by the crowd that it's awfully late and suddenly I am not feeling so well. The pub is full of people and for the first time in my life, I don't want to be around any of them. The walls of the pub begin to close in on me. I actually want to be alone. That is such a new feeling for me; usually I am the party girl, staying out to all hours of the night, but I miss the quiet of Jax's home. I miss the comfort and solitude that I found in his library reading. I miss Jax. Sad, depressed, and very drunk, I decide to return to my room.

I'm not in my room long when there is a knock at the door. *Who in the world could that be? Perhaps Joe has returned and found me?* Too drunk to walk over to the door, I holler, "Come in."

The door opens and in walks the last person I ever believed would be here. *Jax.*

He rushes over to me and kneels down next to the bed, "Oh, Marie! I've been so worried. What are you doing here?"

I'm too drunk to believe in what I am seeing; I believe that I've fallen asleep and I'm having a wonderful dream where Jax comes back to Whitechapel not to save his sister, but to save me. He sweeps me up off my feet, kisses me passionately, and whisks me back to St. James Park.

What a beautiful dream!

I knew you would return.

October 4, 1888

I wake up with a pounding in my head that won't stop. Opening my eyes, I realize that I am not at the Princess Alice and I am indeed back in my room at St. James Park. Next to the bed is a glass of water and a note.

> *My dearest Marie-*
> *You'll need to rehydrate yourself, so please drink the water.*
> *We'll talk when you are feeling better.*
> *Yours, Jax*

I do as I'm told and drink the water. Then I reread the note.

> *Yours, Jax*

I sigh. It wasn't a dream. Jax must have found me last night and brought me here. But why? He should be so angry with me right now. I didn't follow through on our agreement. I was supposed to be back here every night at six. And for the past three nights, I purposely stayed away. I left him. *What time of day is it?* I wonder.

Rising from the bed takes more effort than I had anticipated. *Bloody hell, how much did I drink last night?* I am quickly reminded that before Jax, I spent many days and nights in a drunken stupor. I've even been fined for being drunk and disorderly. Consider it an occupational hazard to deal with the fact that I was selling my body and in most cases, my soul. But since I had been with Jax, I never wanted a drink. I never took one, except for an occasional brandy or glass of wine with Jax. *How odd.*

I walk over to the window gingerly and peek out. The sun is just beginning to set. *Oh my, how long did I sleep?* I walk over to my wardrobe and instead of dressing for any type of meal or actually being seen outside of this suite of rooms, I put on my nightdress and dressing gown. At least it is better than moving about in my undergarments. Did Eliza undress me last night? I must have totally blacked out because I don't remember a thing. Walking over to the door that adjoins my room to Jax's room, I knock. There's no answer. I knock again. Still nothing.

Slowly turning the knob, I open the door. Jax is not in his bedchamber, but I see the soft glow of candlelight from the open door to his sitting room. I walk barefoot across the bedroom to the open doorway. Standing in the doorway, I see Jax sitting in his chair reading the paper, just like always. A smile spreads across my lips. How domesticated this is. This man is not a killer. He's the man I love. I knew that I wanted this life, but I never realized how much until this very moment. He's going to be so angry with me. My heart is going to shatter to pieces when he tells me that he is done with our agreement and me.

His back is to me and I doubt that he knows I am here. I take advantage of this and observe him unnoticed for a minute. He's just as handsome as ever … I can't believe I would think such horrible things about him. I love him. I'm in love with him. *And what if he is this heinous murderer?* my thoughts ask. I shake it off, refusing to answer myself, and say, "Good evening, Jax."

He turns. "You're awake," he says cautiously.

I nod and say, "Yes." It's almost a whisper, as I'm a bit unsure what will happen next.

He pats the seat next to him on the settee and says, "Come and sit with me."

I pad over to him and sit down. He reaches for my hand and takes it into his. "I was so worried about you, Marie."

"I'm sorry." I really have nothing else to say to him. I really can't just blurt out that I thought he was Jack the Ripper and so I ran before he murdered me too.

"Why?" he asks and I can see the hurt in his eyes. "Why did you leave me?" I have really wounded this man and the sight before me breaks my heart. How could I have ever thought he would murder someone, let alone four women?

"Oh Jax, I don't know," I reply. "As soon as I told Jasper to leave me in Whitechapel I regretted it." At least that was the truth.

"But why even entertain it? Was it because I didn't come home the night before?"

"No, no…" I pause uncertainly because I realize that yes, that was part of the reason—I had believed he was out murdering two women. But I don't say that and continue, "I just started having doubts, Jax. Suddenly I needed to be a part of my old life again."

He takes his hand and caresses the side of my cheek ever so gently and I naturally lean my head in to his touch. I love the feel of his fingers against my bare skin and when he caresses me like this and looks at me so lovingly, I am putty in his hands. I am his. I will always be his.

"Jax, kiss me, please."

Pulling me close to him he growls, "Oh God, Marie, I thought you would never ask." And his lips devour mine. They're possessive and demanding, yet at the same time his kiss tells me everything I need to know. He does love me. If he didn't, he would have never brought me back here.

Breaking from our kiss, he asks, "Tell me you are going to stay. Tell me you will never leave me again." The doubts flash back into my mind and I find it hard to answer him. He's giving me everything I want. He is giving me this wonderful life, but I can't forget about the women in Whitechapel. I need time.

"Can we just take it slow, please?" I ask.

He pushes away from me and looks at me incredulously and asks, "You're still unsure? Are you still having doubts? Talk to me. Tell me what you are feeling, please."

I'm silent for a brief moment. I think about what he is asking me and I realize that maybe it might be better for both of us if we do talk about this. Perhaps talking this through will clear up all the confusing doubts that I have.

Nodding, I say, "Alright, we can talk." I pause and then add, "But you must sit over there. When you are this close to me I have trouble thinking straight."

He chuckles as he gets up to move to the chair. "Well, that's a good thing." Sitting down, he says, "Talk." He says it in such a commanding way. When he commands me I don't question anything, I just do as he says. It's one of the things I love so much about him. I don't have to care for myself because he does it for me.

When I'm with Jax, I don't have to make any decisions, I don't have to worry about anything except making him happy, which is very easy to do. He takes all those decision-making burdens away from me and shoulders them all by himself. It's liberating.

"I ran because I was scared and was feeling as if I was suffocating."

"What made you feel that way?" he asks curiously. I can see that he is patiently trying to get me to pinpoint what the one thing was, but hopefully he will see and understand that it was many things.

"Well, it wasn't just one thing. Many things contributed to my fear."

"And what were those things?"

"Two more women were murdered in Whitechapel, on the same night..." I hesitate, but I can see by the look in his eyes that he knows where I'm going with this and he is encouraging me to go on. "On the same night you didn't come home. I guess that would have been the first thing. Those murders are the catalyst. They have drawn me in and it has become an obsession for me to the read the morning paper, just to make sure that nobody else has been murdered. And to add to this mess, I knew Elizabeth Stride. You knew her too." He looks at me curiously. Not giving him a chance to speak, I answer his unspoken question by saying, "That night when you found me after our first encounter, that's who I was sitting with in the Ten Bells. She was my friend."

"Oh my pet, I'm sorry. These murders are unfortunate and I hope they find the sick bastard soon, before anyone else gets hurt." He says that as if he means it, but the ugly face of doubt rears its head again. "What else, Marie?" he asks.

"Well, like I said, it was the same night that you didn't come home."

"But you know about Victoria. I explained to you that I would have to leave periodically to tend to her," he replies.

"Yes, you did. But …" I pause. How can I tell this man who has been nothing but wonderful to me that I believe he is Jack the Ripper?

"Go on, Marie," he coaxes.

I hesitate, "But, the last time you were gone …"

He looks at me curiously, but I can't say the words. We spend a very long moment just staring at each other. And then he totally astounds me by saying, "I think that what you are trying to say is that when Annie Chapman was murdered, I was gone as well. And then, I was also gone the night the other two women were murdered. Right?"

I reply with embarrassment, "Well, yes. It just seems too convenient to me."

"I can see why you would think that, my pet. But I can assure you that it is purely coincidental. I am not a killer, Marie."

I don't say anything. *He sounds sincere, he truly does, but what if I'm just hearing what I want to hear, believing whatever tale he weaves? Do I trust him and take his words as gospel and know that he isn't the killer?*

He gets up from the chair and walks over to the settee. He holds out his hand to me and I hesitantly take it. He pulls me up to stand facing him. "Look at me. Truly look at me, Marie. Look into my eyes," he commands. I look into his soft gray eyes. "Do you see a killer?" he asks.

No. I think it but I don't say it. I see only love, compassion, and empathy in his eyes.

He holds his hands out. "Look at my hands, Marie." I look down at his outstretched hands, as he turns them over and over. "Are these the hands of a killer? Do you see remnants of blood under my nails? You've seen my body, Marie, all of it. What about cuts and scratches, do you see any? Surely if I murdered these women they would have put up a fight, no?" he asks.

Oh God! How could I be so stupid? Jax is not a killer. It is purely coincidental that these murders happened on the nights that he was not with me and that they share the same name. I've been such a fool.

"Oh, Jax, I'm so sorry! I look at you now and I don't know how I could have ever suspected you of such heinous acts. Can you ever forgive me?" I drop to my knees at his feet. The shame of accusing him overwhelms me and I can no longer stand with him as his equal.

He kneels down next to me and pulls my chin up to look at him. "Marie, of course I can forgive you. I can see how you would think such things. You have not known me long and of course you would doubt with so much stacking up against me." He stops talking long enough to kiss my forehead and then my nose and then adds, "My wonderful Marie. Tell me you are home to stay, my love."

"Yes, I am."

He looks at me lovingly and says, "And what do you say to making this arrangement of ours permanent?"

"What?" His last statement astounds me. Is he asking what I think he is asking?

He pulls me against him and holds me in a tight hug. "I don't know how you did it, but you see before you a changed man. I never wanted love. I never intended to fall in love. I even warned you that I would never love you. And look at what you have done to me. I do love you, Marie. I love you more than my own life and when you disappeared I couldn't rest until you were home where you belonged. This is your home now; we can just fuck the agreement. It's you and me now, as it should have always been. Please say you will have me."

"What are you saying?"

"Marry me, Marie. Spend the rest of your life with me, here in my home. Be my wife, my lover, and my friend. Bear my children.

Grow old with me. Everything I never thought I wanted I now want, with you. Tell me you will marry me."

My head is spinning. *Jax loves me and he just asked me to marry him.* I don't need to think about this, I don't need time. I know what's in my heart and what it's been trying to tell me since I first started to doubt him. I love him. "Yes, yes, I will marry you. I love you, Jax."

He leans in and once his lips connect with mine, the heat and passion that we've always shared ignites and suddenly we can't get enough of each other. We don't even get up to go to his bedchamber; we are removing clothes and our hands are greedily exploring each other. Before I know it, Jax has me bent over the settee as he enters me and fills me up. He thrusts urgently, as if he can't get enough of me. He reaches around my front and finds my clit and begins his torturous ministrations to the sensitive bud at my core. The pressure builds and I can feel myself clench around him as I begin my release, screaming his name. I feel him pulse inside me as spurts of hot liquid fill me up. I let go, breathing heavily as I collapse over the settee. His body lazily drapes over mine in pure exhaustion. A few minutes later, naked and fully sated, Jax carries me to our bed. *Our bed. I like the sound of that. Mrs. Jackson Kent. Oh yes, I like the sound of that.*

Waking in the middle of the night, I stretch beside Jax and turn to face him. He is lying on his back and I can see the chiseled muscles of his chest. The urge to touch him overwhelms me and I take a finger and lightly run it through the definition of his abs, tracing tenderly. Once I have traveled through his muscled torso, my finger finds the tuft of hair that trails down to his cock. It is the sexiest thing I have ever seen and I trail my finger to the point of no return, because I know the moment I touch him there, there is no turning back. And I'm good with that.

His cock begins to grow and I know that I now have his attention. His eyes flutter open and he grins. "Don't start something unless you plan to finish it, my pet," he says teasingly, but I also know he is dead serious.

"Oh, Jax," I murmur, my voice thick and huskier than normal.

"Oh, Marie," he whispers as I grab hold of his now-full erection and begin to stroke him. "Will you do something for me?" he asks.

"Of course I will, my love. Anything," I say lovingly.

"Suck me," he commands as he guides my head to his cock. I've been wanting to do this for him since our first time, but he was always in control and never asked. I am elated that he has now asked and I waste no time in grazing his tip with my lips. He hisses with pleasure. I take that as approval and take him completely into my warm, wet mouth. I take him all the way into my throat and he moans. But then he surprises me and grabs my hair, yanking my head away. *Did I do something wrong?*

He gets up from the bed and then pulls me over to the side of the bed. "Lie on your back, Marie, and hang your head over the side of the bed," he commands and I do as I am told. I am not sure what he is planning, but I trust him. I really do. He is standing right where my head hangs and I realize that we are perfectly aligned. All he has to do is slip his cock in my mouth and fuck me. When he slides in, I can feel every part of him. The feeling is consuming as I watch him push in and out of my mouth. He reaches down and rests his hands on my throat and I quickly begin to panic. He says reassuringly, "It's ok, my love, I am just resting my hand on your throat. I like feeling my cock in your throat."

Oh fuck, that was the sexiest thing I have ever heard.

"When I slide in, I want you to try to swallow. Can you do that for me?" he asks.

Of course I can try. He slides back in and I do what he asks. *Holy fuck, I can see that he is coming apart.* I reach up behind my head and latch on to his balls, carefully cupping and caressing them. I feel Jax pulsate in my throat and he comes hard as I swallow every drop of him. When I know that he is completely empty, I lick up any residual cum on his cock.

"Oh God, Marie. You are amazing." As I continue to lick him, he demands, "Touch yourself." He is still towering over me at the side of the bed as I reach down and begin to play with my clit.

"That's it, baby, I need to see your finger swirl around your tight little nub. Are you wet?"

"Yes."

"How wet are you?"

"Very wet," I reply breathlessly.

"Show me. Show me your wetness as it glistens on your finger," he says.

Oh, this is too erotic. I lift my finger to show him the wetness that has formed there.

"Fuck, Marie. Dip it back in and show me again."

"Why don't come here and see for yourself?" I reply. I need him in one form or another between my legs now.

"Is that an order?"

"Yes. Fuck me, Jax."

"How?"

"How? Are you really asking me that now?" I ask.

"Tell me, baby, do you want my cock, my fingers, or my tongue?"

"Oh, my ... your tongue. I want your hot mouth on me now," I cry.

Jax walks over to the other side of the bed and grabs my ankles. He pulls me toward him and places my legs up on his shoulders as he draws me closer to the edge of the bed. He gets down on his knees, bringing his mouth level with my pussy. As the first touch of his tongue sweeps through my slit, I come undone. "Oh yes, just like that." He continues to tease me with his tongue and then he drives it inside me. I begin to literally fuck his face as he continues to suck and eat my core.

He wraps his arms around my thighs, holding me in as his mouth devours my pussy. I grab onto his hair, holding him to me. My climax builds as my body begins to tense and then I explode with the most amazing pleasure as Jax continues to lick and suck me.

He holds me still for several minutes, allowing me to come down from the sensations that have just pulsated through my body

... and then, before I know it, his tongue is replaced with his cock and an incredible feeling of fullness overtakes me. He begins thrusting inside of me, hard, punishing thrusts. I know he's not trying to hurt me, but he is letting go of the heartache of the last few days. I can't believe I was so stupid as to doubt his love. I never thought that this would be the outcome of my actions of a few days ago. This is our new beginning. I have never been happier in my life.

Jax continues to pound into to me. We reach our climax together this time and when he finally slips out of me, he crawls back into bed and snuggles me close up against him. And for the first time since I moved into this house, I wake up exactly like I fell asleep, in Jax's arms. He's here. He didn't leave early in the morning like he normally does. He really is here.

Chapter Fifteen

I snuggle into Jax and he stirs. "Good morning," he says sleepily.

"Good morning," I reply happily. "I like waking up in your arms."

"That's because you are where you belong," he says lovingly as he bends his head down to kiss the top of my head. "But now, you need to get your pretty arse out of bed."

"But why? Can't we stay here all day?" I question petulantly.

"No, definitely not," he replies, shaking his head.

"But why?" I ask again. I know I sound like a petulant child, but I am warm and cozy am basking in the joy of him holding me in our bed. "I never want to leave this bed," I say.

He laughs. "Well, my pet, you can't stay here forever. You have to leave sometime, especially if we are going to get married."

"Married!" I almost forgot. "Are we really getting married?" I ask.

"You did say yes, didn't you?" he asks and then quickly adds, "You can't change your mind."

I look at him with a devilish grin on my face. "Oh no. I'm not changing my mind. You are stuck with me now." I pause and look down.

"What is it?" he asks.

"I just feel as if this is a dream. Like there is no way someone like you would love someone like me. You know what I mean, someone who lives in Whitechapel and does what I do to earn a living. What do the papers call it, the *undesirable class*?"

"Stop. Stop that right now. You are about to be my wife. I don't care where you came from, all I care about is that you are here, now, with me. Understood?"

"Yes, understood."

"So now why don't you get your pretty self up and have Eliza do all those wonderful things she does for you. You and I are going out."

"Out?"

"Yes, we are spending the day together. Just you and me—well, and Carlton, of course." He smirks.

"Well yes, there is Carlton," I add as I giggle. I get up from the bed and scurry, completely naked, over to my room. I open the door that separates our two rooms and hurry in, only to run right into Eliza.

This is a bit awkward. Not awkward that she hasn't seen me naked of course, but awkward because I am naked exiting her Master's bedchamber. But she doesn't flinch in the least and maintains her composure. She's holding a dressing gown up for me to slip in, and as I do she says, "Welcome back, Miss Marie. We sure did miss you."

"Thank you, Eliza. It feels good to be home." I walk over to the dressing table and look at my flush cheeks in the mirror. *Oh well, soon Jax and I will be man and wife and there will not be any need for embarrassment. At least, I hope not.*

"Jax says we are going out today. I shall like to take a bath, then perhaps you can find me something appropriate to wear for a day out and about?"

"Of course. I will order the bath now."

"Thank you, Eliza."

A couple of hours later, I am bathed, coiffed, and dressed for a day out with the man I love. I am convinced that life doesn't get any better than this.

Jax and I return in the early evening. It was a wonderful day, ending with a lovely dinner out at the plaza.

"I'm going to retire. Are you coming?" he asks as we enter the house. He turns to take my wrap and his knuckles gently caress my shoulders. Chills run up and down my spine.

"Yes, let me go change and I'll see you soon."

"I'll send Eliza up." He kisses my hand and then says, "See you soon."

I nod and proceed up the steps.

After Eliza helps me change out of my day clothes and dresses me in my nightclothes and dressing gown, I proceed into Jax's sitting room. He is reading the paper and acknowledges me as I enter.

"Thank you for a lovely day, Jax," I say.

"It was my pleasure. Expect more days like that, my dear."

"You spoil me, Jax. A girl can get used to this."

"Good, I suggest you do because all I want to do is spoil you." He smiles and adds, "Come sit with me. Care to read the *Daily*?"

"Sure. Have they reported anything exciting?"

"Actually, they have had a breakthrough in the Whitechapel murder case."

"Did they catch him?" I ask anxiously.

"No, but they have published a letter that he sent to the Central News Office in London. Apparently he has a name."

"Jack the Ripper," I say in almost a whisper.

"Yes, how did you know that?" he asks, surprised.

"When I was in Whitechapel, I read in the *Daily* that they had received a letter from him and that he was referring to himself as Jack the Ripper."

"Oh. Well, today they have released the letter. Would you like to read it?"

"Yes," I say as I eagerly grab the newspaper that Jax is handing to me. I sit down next to him and begin to read.

Dear Boss,
25 September 1888

I keep on hearing the police have caught me. But they wont fix me just yet. I have laughed when they look so clever and talk about being on the <u>right</u> track. That joke about Leather Apron gave me real fits.

I am down on whores and I shant quit ripping them till I do get buckled. Grand work the last job was. I gave the lady no time to squeal. How can they catch me now? I love my work and want to start again. You will soon hear of me with my funny little games.

I saved some of the proper <u>red</u> stuff in a ginger beer bottle over the last job to write with but it went thick like glue and I can't use it. Red ink is fit enough I hope <u>ha. ha.</u> The next job I do I shall clip the lady's ears off and send to the police officers just for jolly wouldn't you.

Keep this letter back till I do a bit more work. Then give it out straight. My knife's so nice and sharp I want to get to work right away if I get a chance. Good luck.

Yours truly,
Jack the Ripper

Don't mind me giving the trade name
Wasn't good enough to post this before I got all the red ink off my hands curse it. No luck yet. They say I'm a doctor now- <u>ha ha</u>

He laughs. How could he laugh at what he's done? This man is sick and sinister and just the thought of his words send bone-chilling spasms directly through me.

"What do you think?" Jax asks.

"I'm horrified. Reading these words makes him real. I mean, I know he is real, but until now he didn't have a voice. Now he has a voice. What a vile man."

"Yes, he is that. Did you see that they have a possible description of him?"

"No, where?" Jax points to the section and I begin to read.

…the following is a description of the man stated to have been seen in the company with the woman murdered in Berner street, and for whom the police are looking: Age 28; height 5ft 8in; complexion dark; no whiskers; black diagonal coat, hard felt hat, collar and tie; carried a newspaper parcel; was of respectable appearance.

I look over at Jax. Age, height, dark complexion … yes, I would say that Jax is in his late 20s, maybe early 30s, dark complexion, no whiskers, and definitely has a respectable appearance, but he is taller than 5ft 8in. *Stop it, Marie!* I admonish myself. *Quit trying to compare this description to Jax. You both have cleared the air. You know he's not a murderer. He is the man you love. He is the man that will spoil and cherish you for the rest of your life. He's the man you will marry.*

"Are you alright, Marie?" Jax asks and takes me out of my induced haze.

"Oh yes, just a little shaken by all this. I hate that he sent the police a letter, but I truly hope it backfires and it helps them and the Yard to find him."

"Me too. I worry for my sister, just as I am sure that after Elizabeth Stride, you continue to worry for your friends in Whitechapel. Every time I see a headline about another murder in the East End, I fear that it is Victoria. And I can't tell you the relief I feel when I find that it is someone else. I know that sounds a bit selfish and self-serving, but I am human."

"Don't feel that way, I know exactly how you feel. Every time I read those headlines I pray that it is not someone else that I know. And I am just as relieved when it is not. Like you said, we are human and fierce protectors of those we love."

"Thank you for understanding. I was afraid to share those thoughts with you, thinking you might find me cold."

"Not at all. You are just a brother who cares very deeply for his sister. I know you would do anything to help her," I say as I grab hold of his hand and bring it to my lips.

"As I would for you as well. I hope you know that."

I smile. His words warm my heart. "I do now. Thank you for giving me this wonderful life. Thank you for taking a chance on a woman you met in an alleyway."

"I should be thanking you, Marie. You made me feel again. You have given me life and I am addicted. I don't ever want to be without it again."

His words make me sad; I know that he has some sad story in his past that I do not know yet. Though I'm sure he will tell me in time, my impatience gets the best of me and I have to ask. "Jax, what happened? What happened to make you so hardened against love?"

He looks over at me and smiles sadly. "That's a sad story indeed. You don't want to be burdened with my past, Marie, I promise you."

"But I do. Knowing you, your past, all the facets that make you the person that you are makes me feel close to you. Please don't shut me out," I plead.

He looks at me curiously. "You really want to hear my sad story?"

"I really do. Perhaps it will help me understand you better."

"Very well. If we are going to marry, you really should know everything about me." He gets up from the settee and begins to pace, takes a deep breath, and then begins, "When I was seventeen, I was engaged to a woman named Charlotte whom I loved very much. By the time I was eighteen, we were married and expecting our first child. We had love, passion, money and a solid place in London society. There was nothing more we could ever hope or wish for, except for a long marriage and a healthy child. One evening a week or so before Charlotte was to go into her confinement, Victoria had an episode and I was summoned to the East End. I wasn't gone all evening, as her episodes were not as intense as they are now. I was only gone for a few hours, but when I returned home, Charlotte was lying at the bottom of the stairs."

He stops to wipe a tear from his cheek. I reach for him, but he shoos me away. Pacing again, he continues, "There was blood everywhere, and lying next to my wife was the lifeless corpse of my child. She was barely conscious when I reached her. I could not look at my child, I knew I could not save him. It was a boy. My son. But there was a chance to save Charlotte, so I cradled her in my arms and yelled for Rothschild. I screamed until my throat was raw and scratched. Finally, he came into the foyer. Quickly scanning the site before him, he knew exactly what he had to do. There was so much blood, I couldn't tell if she had been stabbed, shot, or what had happened to her. I could only hold her and beg her to hang on to life."

"Oh Jax, I'm so sorry," I say, tears streaming down my face. My heart is breaking for him, Charlotte, and their son. *What could have happened to her? Did she have complications with her pregnancy, or was this another heinous act like the ones in Whitechapel?*

He waved his hand. "Please, Marie. I've started, I must now finish. When the doctor arrived, from the first minute that he walked into the foyer I knew that it wasn't going to end well. I had already lost my son, and now I was going to lose Charlotte as well. We moved her from the entryway to her bedchamber. She was barely breathing. Once she was settled in bed, the doctor looked at me and said, *'Jax, I'm sorry. There is nothing I can do for her. She will not survive the night.'* And he was right. Not thirty minutes later she was dead. After my son and Charlotte were buried, I moved out of the house she and I had shared and into this house. I couldn't live in the house in which I'd lost everything and I swore I would never love again."

"Did you ever find out what happened to her?" I ask, silent tears falling like rain down my face.

"The doctor suspected that she went into labor early, and with no one to help her, she delivered her baby on her own and bled out. My son was born too early to survive." He sits back down next to me. I reach over and wrap my arms around him, holding him close.

"Thank you for telling me," I say and then I add, "I love you so much, Jax. Please don't ever forget that."

He reaches his hand up to hold on to my arms that are wrapped around him. "I love you too, Marie, very much."

We sit like that for several minutes and then Jax says, "Come on, love, let's go to bed."

I nod and follow him into the bedroom. Crawling into bed, I snuggle up against him and eventually fall asleep in his arms.

Chapter Sixteen

October 30, 1888

The rest of the month passes by so quickly that I have to stop several times to catch my breath. Jax and I spend much more time together. The banns for our marriage have been read and I want nothing more than to be his wife.

As we both sit down to breakfast this morning, Jax says, "So, my dear, tell me what kind of wedding you would like. It can be as simple or as ostentatious as you would like." He grins.

Ever since I returned back to St. James, Jax and I have had breakfast together every morning, except for two—both instances where he needed to go to Whitechapel and tend to his sister, again. And to my relief, there were no murders in Whitechapel during his absence. Actually, it has been a whole month with no murders. The killing spree has ended and I couldn't be more relieved. My heart is so full. I am marrying a man that I love beyond reason, beyond any more doubts. Especially doubts that he is a killer.

"I would like a simple and small wedding, perhaps just us." He doesn't say anything in response and I feel compelled to continue talking. "We've both been married before and I don't think we need all the pomp and circumstance that is required from a society wedding. What do you think?"

He looks over at me and smiles. "I couldn't agree more. Simple it is, just us and perhaps a few witnesses to make it legal," he adds.

I rise from my chair and jump over to hug him. "Thank you, Jax."

He chuckles and I add, "Would you do one more thing for me?"

"Of course, my pet. Anything."

"Would you take me back to Whitechapel?" I had been contemplating this for about a week now; I need to sever all my ties there. I need to speak with Joe and say goodbye to my friends. There are a few people there that I care about and I feel bad about just disappearing.

"Why on earth would you want to go back there?" he asks.

"To say goodbye. To tie up loose ends," I reply.

"Do you really feel that is necessary?"

"I do. I need to see Joe one last time. I need to thank him for trying to provide for me as best he could. I need to thank Madam Grace for taking me under her wing. She gave me a way to earn a living and I can't forget that. And I have a few friends, too: Julia and Mrs. Harvey. Please, Jax," I plead.

"Of course, of course we can go back. But you are not going alone. Are you comfortable with me accompanying you?" he asks.

"Yes, of course. Perhaps you can introduce me to your sister?" I add.

"Yes, perhaps," he says sadly.

"Jax, is everything alright?" I ask.

"I'm sorry, Marie. It's just that we have lost her. My men have always done a good job of keeping tabs on her, but since her last episode, we have not been able to locate her. It's as if she has vanished."

"Oh Jax, I am so sorry," I reply. I can see that he is worried and I wish there was something I could do to help him. And then the idea pops in my head. "Perhaps my friends may know her. When we go back to Whitechapel today, maybe someone I know might have seen her."

"You know, I didn't think about that. When she has disappeared in the past, I have never really had someone on the inside that could help. This might be the answer." He hesitates and then asks, "Are you sure you are comfortable with this?"

Ripper

"Of course! After all you have done for me, it is the least I can do. Actually, it brings me joy to know that I can finally do something for you," I reply.

He strokes my cheeks and says, "But Marie, you are wrong. You do something for me every day. You love me unconditionally. A man like me could not ask for anything more."

We finish our breakfast and Jax calls for Carlton to prepare the carriage. It occurs to me that I have not seen Jasper since my return. *Oh, I hope that he has not lost his job!* I have not needed to go out on my own because since my return, Jax has always gone out with me. He still leaves in the mornings on most days and returns around dinnertime, but I have been so content in the quiet of *our home* that I have not had the desire to go out. The restlessness that I experienced before is long gone.

Once we are settled in the carriage and heading to Whitechapel, I ask, "Jax, I have not seen Jasper since I've been back. Is he still in your employ?" I ask.

"Of course he is. I did think about relieving him of my employ when he left you in Whitechapel, but he was the one who helped me find you and for that I am forever grateful to him."

"Oh, I'm so glad. I didn't want him to lose his livelihood because of me. Thank you." My arm is intertwined with his and I squeeze it ever so gently. "Is he still my coachman?" I ask.

"Yes, he is and he has strict instructions to never leave you anywhere away from me." He chuckles. I love his possessiveness. I find it curious that I detested Joe's possessiveness, but Jax's I welcome without a thought otherwise.

When we arrive at the curb of Dorsett Street, Carlton works his way down from his post and opens the side door. Jax gets out and then reaches his hand inside for me. I take it and make my way from the carriage. "Shall I come with you?" Jax asks.

"Will you?" I ask. Suddenly I don't want to face this alone; having him there with me gives me the strength that I didn't know I needed until now.

"Of course I will," he says as he takes my arm.

We make our way to the door and I knock. "Who is it?" I hear Joe's voice from the other side of the door.

"It's Marie," I say.

As he opens the door, he says, "Well, the prodigal harlot has returned home." But then he stops when he sees I am not alone. He then adds, "And you must be the arse that took her away in the first place."

Jax says, "Mister Joe—I'm sorry I don't know your last name—I think you need to calm down and let Marie talk. There are some things that she would like to say to you and you need to give her the chance to say them."

"Who the fuck do you think you are?" Joe yells. "No high-society arse is going to tell me what to do!" Joe reaches for Jax aggressively, but in one swift move Jax wards him off and Joe ends up against the wall, held there by Jax.

"You listen to me, you worthless piece of shit. You will sit down in that chair over there and you will listen to what the lady has to say. And when she is done, we will leave here and never come back. Am I understood?" I have never seen Jax in such a state and I have to say, I really like it. Joe nods and Jax releases him. He walks over to the chair and sits.

"Talk," he says.

I look over to Jax and he nods. I walk farther into the room and say, "I wanted to apologize for everything and say thank you for all that you have done for me before I met Jax."

"Are you done?" Joe replies sullenly.

I know he is hurt and angry. I understand his hurt and anger. "Joe, I know you feel I have used you, and perhaps I have. You knew from the beginning that I never loved you. Not the way you loved me. I was always searching ... and with Jax, I have found what I've always needed."

I could see him soften as the tears begin to pool in his eyes. "But I love you, Marie," he pleads.

I kneel down in front of him and say, "I know. I know you do, and I am so sorry that I hurt you. But I have to follow my heart,

Joe. You of all people would want that for me, wouldn't you?" He nods. I lean in and kiss him on the cheek. I whisper, "I'll never forget you and everything that you did for me." I get up and turn to Jax. "I'm ready to go." Jax nods and opens the door.

As we turn and begin to make our way out, I am startled by a loud crash. I turn and find that Joe has punched holes in the window by the door, breaking two window panes. Blood is dripping from his hands from all the cuts and scratches. "Joe!" I exclaim as I run to him, grabbing a cloth from the table to tend to the blood.

Jax comes to my aid and says, "Here, let me." He takes over tending to Joe's hand.

Joe scoffs and says, "I'm fine. Will you both just leave? I don't need any help from either of you."

"But Joe, you are hurt!"

"Marie, please just go."

I look at Jax and nod. My being here is only hurting Joe more.

Joe says, "By the way, Marie, I am leaving town. I'm moving as far away as I can from London. I'll be staying with Mrs. Buller until my passage from London is finalized. I can't stay here anymore. The room is paid for the next two months. So if any of your cronies need a place, it's yours to do with what you like." He pauses for a moment and then adds, "Now if you will just go, please."

Jax and I leave. I find that I am glad that Joe is leaving London and all the memories that go with it. Hopefully he will find a good life away from this hellhole and find some happiness. All in all, he is a good man and deserves to be happy.

Once we are outside, Jax asks, "Are you alright, my pet?"

"Yes, I needed to do that. Thank you."

He takes my hand and kisses it, then says, "Where to next?"

"The Ten Bells," I say. I am sure that is where I will find Julia and Mrs. Harvey.

"Would you like to walk?" he asks.

"I would, thank you." And then I realize that I never asked Joe about Victoria. "Jax, we forgot about Victoria!" I say.

"I didn't; I just felt it best not to hurt the man more than we already have. He's a broken man, Marie, and until you came along, I knew exactly how that felt. Whether he knows about Victoria or not, I decided that it was best not to pursue more conversation with him. He needs to be left alone tending to his wounds, and not just the ones on his hands."

"Oh." I understand his reasoning, but I really want to help him and I know that Joe knows a lot of people in the district. I guess there is always Julia, Madame Grace, and Mrs. Harvey. They may know something.

We walk toward the Ten Bells Pub, which is a few blocks down from my old building, across from the Spitalfields Market. Once we arrive, the memories of this place haunt me. This was my stomping ground, where I acquired work and drank my sorrows away. But no more. Today, I arrive as the future Mrs. Jackson Kent.

Walking in the pub, I spot Julia and Mrs. Harvey together over in the corner sharing a drink. I yank on Jax's shoulder and point to the corner. He nods and we make our way over to them.

As we approach, Julia says, "Well well, look who we 'ave 'ere." Mrs. Harvey remains silent, she was always the more well-bred of the two.

"Hello, may we join you?" I ask.

Mrs. Harvey slides over and makes room for us. Jax pulls up a chair and we sit. "So what brings Miss High-and-Mighty back to Whitechapel?" Julia says.

"Julia, please. I know what you think of me, but I do not believe I am better than either one of you or anyone here in the East End. I lived this life and I know where I've come from. Don't punish me because I met Jax."

"So, that's 'is name," she says.

"Yes, this is Jackson Kent."

Mrs. Harvey nods and says, "It is nice to meet ya, Mr. Kent. I can tell by the smile on Marie's face that you make her very happy. My best wishes to ya both." She picks up her drink in a toast-like fashion and then takes a swig.

"I just wanted to come by and say goodbye to you both. The three of us have been through a lot together and I just wanted you both to know that you were such a huge part of my life," I say, hoping to melt the icy stare that Julia give me.

She nods and says, "Aw, go on Marie. I'm sorry for being such a bitch to ya. I guess I'm just jealous. We all want what you and Mr. Kent have found." She looks over to him and then adds, "At least he's nice to look at and not an old man." She pauses and then adds, "Remember when Lucy left with that really rich guy that was like thirty years her senior? Christ, he was an old man!" They both giggle and I can't help but laugh. I do remember that and we all just laughed at what kind of life she would have, even if it did get her out of Whitechapel.

Jax grunts as if the conversation is a bit uncomfortable for him and I realize that we need to move on. But before we go, there are questions that need to be asked. "Before I forget, do you ladies know a Victoria Kent?"

Julia speaks up and says, "I know a Vickie, but I don't know her last name."

"What does she look like?" Jax asks eagerly.

"She's about Marie's height, dark hair, really pretty when she's not strung out on opium," Julia says.

Jax looks at me and says, "That's her!" Then he turns to my friends and says, "When was the last time you saw her?"

"Last night," Mrs. Harvey replies.

"Last night? Where?" Jax asks.

"Madam Grace's," Julia replies. "She was getting work for the night, just like the rest of us." I see Jax's heart break. I had assumed that she was prostituting, but I guess it was the last thing Jax expected. The disappointment that has taken over his face breaks my heart to pieces. But really, she had to support her addiction somehow. To me, it was an obvious conclusion.

Jax turns to me and says, "Shall we go see Madam Grace?"

"Yes," I reply. I turn back toward Julia and Mrs. Harvey and say, "My old flat is available for the next two months. Joe is leaving

Whitechapel and has paid for the place through the end of the year in the event that I came back. Since I won't be coming back, you both are more than welcome to utilize it. I know how hard it can be to find a place for the night."

"Oh, Marie!" Mrs. Harvey exclaims, "Thank you!"

"I no longer have a key, but Joe punched out the window pane next to the door. You can just reach in and open the spring latch. You shouldn't have any problems." I get up to leave and Jax follows suit. "I'll miss you both. We've had some memorable times, the three of us. Take care of yourselves," I say as I turn to leave.

"It was very nice to meet you both," Jax adds. "We will be living in St. James. You both are more than welcome to come and visit Marie whenever you like. Just send word and she can have her coachman to come and collect you."

I look at Jax in astonishment. Did he really just invite them to St. James to visit us, whenever they want?

"That is really kind of you, Mr. Kent. I can see what Marie sees in you," Julia says.

As Jax and I walk out of the pub, I stop just outside the door. "I cannot believe you just did that," I say.

"What did I just do?" he asks.

"You just invited two known prostitutes to your home to visit your future wife who used to be one as well. Aren't you worried about scandal?"

He laughs. "No, my love, I am not worried about scandal. My worries about scandal and I parted company many years ago. The only thing I worry about is making my wife happy. And if seeing her old friends makes her happy, then so be it."

I shake my head. "You are just too good to be true." We turn to the doorway of the Ten Bells that leads upstairs as we make our way to Madam Grace's.

Once we get to the top of the stairs, the old familiar scent of treated wood, lingering alcohol, and stale smoke fills my nose. I realize that all I want to do is get out of here, but I have come here to say my goodbyes—and of course to help Jax. So, I push on toward Madame Grace's room. I knock. "Who is it?" she says from the other side of the door.

"Marie and Mr. Kent," I reply.

Opening the door with a smile on her face, she says, "I wondered when I might see you again. Please, come in." As we step into her room, she adds, "What brings you both here?"

"We're getting married," I blurt out. I hadn't intended on telling her that way, but I was anxious to show her I was moving on to a better life.

"Oh joy!" she exclaims. "I couldn't be more pleased." She comes over and gives me a hug and then adds, "You were one of my best girls, Marie. I shall miss you." She looks over to Jax warily and then adds, "And if things don't work out, you always have a place here."

"Grace, I thank you for that, but I really don't think that will be an issue," I say as I reach for Jax's hand as he takes mine so naturally. *How could anyone think that things will not work out for us?*

"I know, I know. But you know how I worry about my girls. I just want you to know you always have a place. That's all. I'm not trying to place doom and gloom on your love that obviously shines so bright."

"Thank you. We've also come for another reason, if you have a minute," I say.

"Of course. What can I do for you?"

I look to Jax, who replies, "Well madam, I believe that my sister may be in your employ. I have been trying to find her for a week now and have not been successful. Do you happen to know a Victoria Kent?"

Grace smiles and then says, "I do. She started working for me about two weeks ago. Great girl, but she has problems, as I am sure you know, sir."

"I do," Jax replies. "I usually have men who keep an eye on her, but they lost sight of her over a week ago and I have been consumed with worry." He pauses and then adds, "So she is well?"

"As well as anyone can be with her addiction. Would you like to see for yourself?"

"She is here?"

"Yes, she stayed here last night. She should be finishing up shortly and she will report to me before she leaves. Would you like some tea while you wait?" she asks.

"If you don't mind us waiting, yes, we would like that," Jax replies as he helps me with my wrap.

"Please sit. I shall return shortly."

After Grace leaves the room, I turn to Jax. "How are you?" I worry for him. Ever since he found out what his sister had been doing to earn a living, I can see the heartbreak all over his face.

"I am fine and very glad that we have found her. I'm just worried about her state of mind when she comes here."

I reach over and take his hand. "I know, but we will face this together. You no longer have to deal with her and all this alone. I am here for you forever and always." He squeezes my hand but doesn't reply.

A few minutes later, Grace returns with a tray. Setting it down on the table before us, she begins to pour. "Milk and sugar?" she asks. We both nod and she proceeds to prepare our tea. This moment is so surreal for me. In all the years that I have known Grace, worked for Grace providing her a steady income, I have never sat in her room and had tea. "Vickie should be here within the hour."

After an hour passes, our tea long gone, I see that Jax is getting antsy. He begins to pace the room. "Jax darling, please sit down. I know you are anxious, but I am sure Victoria will be here any minute." I know how these things go. You get with a man who wants you to linger, he wants one more kiss, one more touch, one more anything to keep you with him longer than you were paid to be. I don't dare explain this to Jax. He is already feeling out of sorts by this whole thing and the last thing I need to be doing is giving him a detailed account of what goes on with a John. The less he knows about that, the better.

Jax does not listen to me and continues to pace. Grace and I make small talk to pass the time. A few minutes later, there is a knock at the door. "Ah, there she is," she says to us quietly. A little louder, she addresses the door, "Who is it?"

"It's Vickie, Madam Grace." When Jax hears her voice he stops pacing and I can see the relief wash over him. It's definitely her.

"Come in," Grace says and the door begins to open. Jax stays rooted in place as Victoria enters the room.

She walks right into the room. She sees me and gives me a polite nod and then goes straight to Madame Grace. She pays Jax no mind; I am sure she hasn't noticed his presence yet. "I'm so sorry I'm late, Madam Grace. I tried to get away, but he kept insisting. However, I did earn an extra 2d."

"Good girl," Madam Grace says. Before she can say another word, Jax finally speaks.

"Hello, Victoria," Jax says. Victoria stops and slowly turns, first looking at me sitting in the chair and then her eyes go straight to her brother, standing off to the side. They lock eyes and it occurs to me that Victoria is lucid, not high—I get the feeling that Jax has not seen her like this in a long time.

"Jackson," she whispers. "What are you doing here?" she asks with shame and embarrassment on her face.

He walks over to her and takes her hands. "I was worried about you."

"Why were you worried?" she asks.

"Well, Victoria, the last time I saw you ... well, let's just say you were not yourself. And then I lost track of you."

"The last time you saw me?" she questions. "Jackson, we have not seen each other since you laid dear Charlotte to rest." Jax cringes as her words force him to remember a painful memory that still cuts him like a knife.

"Victoria, I was with you just last week. Don't you remember?" he pleads.

Oh, how awful. She must have been in such a state that she doesn't remember him being with her or helping her.

"Jackson, I really don't know what you are talking about. But as you can see, I am doing just fine. Madam Grace has given me employment and I am doing very well. But thank you for your concern," she states rather rudely.

"Victoria, come home with me. You know I will provide for you. I will take care of you and give you anything you need. Please, you don't have to remain here," he begs.

"I choose to stay here, Jackson. The last place I want to be is with you. You blamed me for Charlotte and your son. You said it was entirely my fault and that I was as dead to you as they were. Your words destroyed me and made me the woman I am today."

He flinches. I remember him telling me that he had been out tending to Victoria when Charlotte and his son died. I can see how he could blame her, but he is obviously trying to make amends. *How on earth can she be so cold to him? Can't she see he is doing what he can to make up for such cold and hateful words?*

He says, "Victoria, that was a long time ago. I don't deny I said those words to you and I have never forgiven myself since then. But allow me to make it up to you. I can give you a better life." He pauses and when she doesn't answer he adds, "I'm getting married again." He gestures over to me and says, "This is Marie, my future wife. I think you both would get on well and I think it would be good for you to have another woman influencing your life."

He reaches for her, but she shifts and pushes him away. "It's too late, Jackson. I will never go back to society. I like it here. I can be myself and I don't have to worry about anyone placing judgment on me. Go on. Get married and have a happy life. I hope it ends better than the last marriage," she says as she storms out.

Jax sighs. "Well, at least I tried."

I get up from my chair and walk over to him. "Oh Jax, I'm so sorry. Maybe after she has time to think she will change her mind."

He shrugs. "Maybe," he says and then adds, "You know, that was the first time I have seen her lucid in years. It was the first time that I could really talk to her and she could hear and understand me." I give him a hug and hold him close. "Well, Madam Grace, I think we should be going."

"Goodbye, Master Kent. I'm sorry that things did not go better for you and your sister," Grace says.

"Me too." He reaches in his pocket and pulls out a card. "Here is my calling card. If Victoria ever needs me, or if she changes her mind and wishes to find me, this is my address." He hands the card to Grace and looks at me. "Are you ready to go, my dear?"

"Yes. Let's go home, Jax," I say and I mean it. This place holds nothing more for me and I am ready to start my new life with Jax.

Chapter Seventeen

November 7, 1988

Jax and I have developed a new routine now. He spends more time at home and we are always together. Everything is different from when I first moved in. He is home more often than not and he constantly dotes on me. We have the most amazing times together. Tonight we have had a lovely dinner. We spent an hour or so in the sitting room, reading over the news of the day and talking about our future. Now we are alone in our bedchamber.

I'm lying naked on the bed and Jax is stalking around the bed commanding me.

"Touch yourself, Marie," he commands. My eyes never leaving his, I reach down and begin to touch myself. "Good girl," he praises. "Rub that clit for me, my pet. Make yourself nice and wet for my cock," he says.

I moan at his words. *Oh God, I love it when he talks to me like this.*

"Now take one finger and position it just at the entrance of your pussy." I do as he says and he praises me again. "Yes, good girl." He begins pacing around the bed and I can see beads of sweat form on his face. His hand is wrapped firmly around his cock, holding himself securely as he commands me to do his bidding. The power that my submission has over him is intoxicating. It is such an illusion. I may be doing everything he tells me, obeying his every command, but it is me that wields the power over him. I realize as I watch him come undone by my obedience that I am the one in control and he knows it.

"Now push two fingers inside," he commands. Again, I do what he says as he begins to stroke his cock. "That's it, just like that," he says. "Does that feel good, my pet? Are you wet for me?" he asks.

"Oh God, yes. I want you, Jax. Please?" I beg.

"Do you have any idea how breathtakingly beautiful you look right now? Touching yourself while your eyes beg for my cock?"

"Please Jax, please," I beg some more.

"Should I let you cum on your fingers or my cock, Marie?"

"Your cock, please." I wait for him to do something to sate my desire, but he does nothing. "I want your cock, Jax."

"Now?" he asks.

"Yes, please," I beg. He's driving me insane with want. But he is the master tease, always making me beg him for more, for everything.

"Keep moving those fingers in and out of you and let me watch you cum and then maybe I will give you my cock."

I don't even respond. Knowing that I'm going to get what I want just from pleasuring myself, I move my fingers harder and faster and within seconds I am convulsing through my orgasm. He doesn't even give me time to come down from the sensations pulsating within me. He is on top of me, pushing my fingers away from my pussy and thrusting his cock inside of me. *Oh yes! That is what I needed.* "Jax, you feel so good."

It didn't take long for my body to begin to tremble. I scream out as my orgasm takes hold of me and in the throes of my ecstasy, I feel Jax pulsate inside of me, stretching and filling me with his cum. It doesn't get any better than this.

My life is a fairy tale and I never want to leave it.

As we lie there sated and spent from our lovemaking, I curl into Jax and snuggle close. "I need to leave early in the morning," he says.

"Oh," I reply. "Is everything alright?"

"Yes, everything is fine, my pet. I just need to take care of some business in town in the morning."

It occurs to me that I don't know what he does for a living. *Does he work, or is he a landowner? I guess I never thought to ask.* Too tired to think about it now, I make a mental note to ask him tomorrow. I slowly drift off to sleep and dream about the glorious fairy tale that my life has become.

The next morning I wake to an empty bed. Jax told me that he wouldn't be here when I woke, that he had to be gone in the morning. Stretching and yawning after another well-rested night, I slowly make my way out of bed and into my bedchamber. Eliza is not here yet this morning and I relish the peace and quiet. I sit down on the bed, trying to remember if I have ever been so completely and incandescently happy. *Never. Until now.* I realize that since my return to St. James, I have only slept in this room one night and that was my first night back. I was so drunk that night that I don't even remember being put to bed. But I remember waking to Jax's note. It still rests on the nightstand with the empty glass of water that he had left for me. I pick it up lovingly and read it again.

> *My dearest Marie-*
> *You'll need to rehydrate yourself, so please drink the water.*
> *We'll talk when you are feeling better.*
> *Yours, Jax*

I look at his beautiful handwriting. It's lovely and elegant. *Is there anything about this man that isn't?* I ask myself. Tracing my finger over the beautiful cursive letters, a realization comes over me that drops fear and panic into every part of my being. *Where have I seen that handwriting before?"*

I frantically run back to the sitting room and start rummaging through the newspapers that we have stacked in there. *October 20, October 18, October 5 … Oh God, where is it,* I think while I move the papers that I have seen to the side. *Please let me be wrong about this. Please let me be chasing illusions again.* Suddenly, there it is, staring me right in the face as if to say "I told you so." October 3, right on the front page: the Dear Boss letter.

> *Dear Boss,*
> *25 September 1888*
> *I keep on hearing the police have caught me. But they wont fix me just yet. I have laughed when they look so clever and talk about being on the <u>right</u> track. That joke about Leather Apron gave me real fits.*
>
> *I am down on whores and I shant quit ripping them till I do get buckled. Grand work the last job was. I gave the lady no time to squeal. How can they catch me now? I love my work and want to start again. You will soon hear of me with my funny little games.*
>
> *I saved some of the proper <u>red</u> stuff in a ginger beer bottle over the last job to write with but it went thick like glue and I can't use it. Red ink is fit enough I hope <u>ha. ha.</u> The next job I do I shall clip the lady's ears off and send to the police officers just for jolly wouldn't you.*
>
> *Keep this letter back till I do a bit more work. Then give it out straight. My knife's so nice and sharp I want to get to work right away if I get a chance. Good luck.*
>
> *Yours truly*
> *Jack the Ripper*
> *Don't mind me giving the trade name*
> *Wasn't good enough to post this before I got all the red ink off my hands curse it. No luck yet. They say I'm a doctor now- <u>ha ha</u>*

The image in the paper is hard to read, but the writing is similar. Too similar. Carrying the paper with me, I run back to my room and grab the note. I compare the handwriting and to my horror they are extremely similar. *Without a doubt they are the same. The same man wrote both of these letters. Jax is Jack the Ripper.*

It can't be.

No, I will not believe this.

I look again. There are places where they are different, but there are also places where they are the same. *Oh God, what should I do?* Tears begin to fall and I cannot stop crying. I begin shaking and convulsing, trying to catch my breath.

I am beyond any rational thought as I come to the realization that all my fears were justified. He lied to me to protect himself. And then the worst feeling consumes me as I wonder, *Is he planning on killing me?*

I have to get out of this house. I need to get as far away as I can from him. I need to go to the police and report him. Oh God, I can't do that. I love him.

My head is spinning. *Marie, get a hold of yourself. You need to think rationally.* I take a deep breath and say aloud, "Marie, before you do anything else, you need to leave here."

I get myself dressed quickly and then rip the Dear Boss letter from the paper and hurry downstairs and head toward the dayroom. Rothschild is standing at the door. "Breakfast, Miss Marie?" he asks.

Calmly, because I don't want to alarm the staff, I say, "No, Rothschild. I won't be eating breakfast this morning. But I would like Jasper to prepare my carriage. I need to run out for a bit, please."

"Of course, miss."

"Thank you."

A few minutes later Rothschild returns to tell me that Jasper is waiting outside for me. "Thank you again, Rothschild." I realize that I will not be returning and I walk over to him and give him a hug. I know it's not proper, but I like him and I am sorry that he works for such a heinous man. "Thank you," I repeat and leave the room.

Jasper is waiting on the curb next to the carriage, the door open and waiting for me. "Where to, Miss Marie?" he asks.

"Whitechapel, please." He looks at me warily. The last time he took me to Whitechapel it almost got him fired. "Jasper, it's fine, I promise," I reassure him.

"Very well then." He moves to his post and off we go.

Once we arrive in Whitechapel, he stops at the usual spot, comes down from his post, and comes around to open the carriage door. "We're here, miss."

I reach for his hand as he helps me out. "Thank you, Jasper."

"Miss, are you unwell?" he asks.

I look at him fondly. "No Jasper, I'm not unwell, but things are not good. They are about as bad as they can be." I pause for a moment and then I add, "Jasper, you need to get away from Master Kent. Find another employer and get as far away from him as you can. He's a bad man, Jasper. He has hurt many people and he will eventually hurt you," I say.

Jasper looks at me dubiously and says, "Miss Marie, you are so wrong about him. He is the kindest man I know. He would never hurt anyone."

"Jasper, you are blinded. I know better, I have proof. I have proof that he is Jack the Ripper. Get away from him!" I exclaim.

"Oh miss, you are so wrong."

"Jasper, I have proof. Look!" I take out the note and the page I ripped from the paper. "The handwriting is the same."

He looks at both the note and the Dear Boss letter. "Miss Marie, your eyes are deceiving you. The handwriting is not the same," he says.

"I'm sorry, Jasper. I don't want to believe it either. I still love him. But I have to do what is in my heart. Go home, Jasper, and if you are smart you will heed my advice."

"But Miss Marie…" he says and I hold up my hand to stop him. I'm done listening to anything he has to say. I don't want to hear any more and I need him to leave. I know that Jax will come after me, especially because I can identify him. So I have to quickly bury myself deep in the East End, where Jackson Kent will never find me.

I give Jasper a hug and run off. Tears are streaming down my face at the loss of the life that I almost had with the love of my life. My heart is broken and my world is shattered.

I run toward the Ten Bells Pub. *Grace can hide me. She will make sure I am safe.*

Once I get to the pub, I head straight upstairs looking for Grace. I am told that she has gone out and should return shortly. I tell the girl that gives me the information to let her know that I need to see her and that I am downstairs at the pub. I give her my name and head down to the bar.

I begin to drink.

I drink more than I should.

Grace never comes down and I wonder what has detained her. Julia appears and we start drinking together. I think about telling her why I am drowning my sorrows in whisky, but then I change my mind. She would never believe me anyway.

Soon, my love, I shall have your heart

Chapter Eighteen

November 9, 1888

    It's after midnight and Julia and I have been drinking since 8 pm. We are extremely drunk and it feels so good to be numb. Isn't that what one does when their life is over? Don't they drown their sorrows in alcohol when their heart is breaking and there is no way to mend it? Isn't this what one does when they want to die?

    "Come on, Marie, let's change the scene and go down to the Horn of Plenty," Julia says.

    Realizing that at this point Grace will not be returning tonight and I will have to talk to her tomorrow, I reply, "Yes, we definitely need a new atmosphere."

    We spend some time at the Horn and then move on to the Britannia. I am sure that Jax is looking for me by now and the fact that we are moving around is working to my favor.

    After too many drinks and pubs to count, I decide that I need to go somewhere and sleep this off. I will have a fresher mind and will able to run more effectively by morning. I will go back to my flat. If Jax is out looking for me, which I am sure he is, my flat is the last place he would look. I'm sure he would scour the pubs first, since that is where he found me the last time, so I'm pretty confident that I am safe for the time being.

    As I walk down Dorset Street toward my home, I break out in song. I do this every time I am drunk like this and although I have nothing to sing about, I belt out the saddest melody. I have no idea of the hour, but I know that it is well past three, maybe even four in the morning. I really don't know and I realize I really don't care. Turning down toward Miller's Court, I come to what had been my home with Joe.

I no longer have a key, so I hope that Joe is there. But then I remember about the broken window. I reach through the window and undo the lock. The door opens slowly and I am surprised by what greets me as I enter the dark room.

"What are you doing here?" I ask the man sitting at my table.

He rises from the chair and begins to approach me. "I've come for you," he replies. I know who he is and I know why he's here and surprisingly enough, I am calm. I should have known all along that this would lead to me. *Oh, how foolish I've been. To think I could run from him.* I should be afraid; I should be terrified by his presence. But I'm not afraid. I'm fully prepared for what my fate is to be. But before he begins his ghastly deed, I must speak to him. I need answers.

"Are you ..." I can't even get the words out. I know the answer, but hearing him say it aloud will make it real, make him real. *What have I done? I've caused so much damage and so many innocent people have died. I should have known all along that this was about me. Why was I too blind to see it?*

Because you are self-absorbed and selfish, Marie, that's why, my consciousness silently cries out.

"You want to know if I'm the Ripper?" he asks, pulling his knife from his cloak. "What do you think, Marie?"

I nod, because I know that he is. "And you have come for me?" I ask. "I thought you ..."

He doesn't let me finish and says, "Surely you knew that you would be next."

"But it's been over a month since your last victim!" I exclaim. "Why murder more when you've gotten away with it?" I ask. "And why didn't you just come for me in the first place?"

He chuckles. "A serial killer never stops killing until he is caught. You've known that all along." He pauses and then adds coldly, "Besides, stopping would ruin all the fun."

"Fun? You call these gruesome murders fun? Those poor women ... how could you?"

"Oh Marie, you surprise me. You knew I wouldn't stop and you knew I'd be coming for you. Didn't you? Deep down in the depths of your soul, you've always known it was I. You questioned, you doubted, you even accused an innocent man unjustly. But deep down, you knew. That's why you kept coming back here. Subconsciously, you came to find me. Somehow you knew I would eventually be waiting for you right here." His voice is sultry and sinister all the same time. This man is pure evil and I can't believe that I actually cared about him at one point in my life.

"Now be a good girl and let me do what I came here to do. I need you to make this easy, Marie. Submit to me."

"What if I don't?" I ask defiantly. I know my defiance will be short-lived. I have never been able to stand up this man.

"Marie, you know better than to play power games with me. You know that all I have to do is command you and like the good little pet that you are, you will obey." He pauses and then commands calmly, "Lie on the bed, Marie."

Just as he said, without any hesitation, I do as he asks and lie on the bed. He takes the knife and holds it to my throat. "Anything you want to say before you can no longer talk?" he asks.

"I'm sorry for all the pain I caused you," I say and he takes the knife and slices my throat.

And as the last ripples of blood course through my veins, at least I have no more doubts or fear. I doubt he will kill again; like he says, this was all about me. *Will they ever catch him?* I doubt that as well.

Everything is so clear now, all of the questions finally answered. Now I understand why I was so captivated and consumed by these murders. They were personal. I knew all along who the murderer was, I had just refused to see it.

But at least I now know—without any doubts—that Jax is *not* the Ripper.

As I begin to lose consciousness, I have only one regret. I'm sure that Jasper told Jax why I left. He will think I believed him to be a murderer.

Jax will be devastated, hurt, and so confused. After all the hearts I have broken in the past, it's finally time for my own to shatter into a million pieces for what I have done. I finally know what it's like to feel remorse for my actions.

I'm so sorry, Jax.
The fairy tale is over.

Epilogue

Times (London)
Saturday, November 10, 1888

ANOTHER WHITECHAPEL MURDER

During the early hours of yesterday morning, another murder of a most revolting and fiendish character took place in Spitalfields. This is the seventh which has occurred in this immediate neighborhood, and the character of the mutilations leaves very little doubt that the murderer in this instance is the same person who committed the previous ones, with which the public is fully acquainted.

The scene of this last crime is at 26 Dorset Street, Spitalfields, which is about 200 yards from 29 Hanbury Street where the previous victim Annie Chapman was so foully murdered. The victim's name is Mary Jane Kelly, though she also went by Mary Jane or Marie Kelly. The entrance to her room at 26 Dorset Street is up a narrow court, in which are some half-a-dozen houses, and which is known as Miller's Court; it is entirely separated from the other portion of the house, and has an entrance leading into the court...

...a horrible and sickening sight presented itself. The poor woman lay on her back on the bed, entirely naked. Her throat was cut from ear to ear, right down to the spinal column. The ears and nose had been cut clean off. The breasts had also been cleanly cut off and placed on a table which was at the side of the bed. The stomach and abdomen had been ripped open, while the face was slashed about, so that the features of the poor creature were beyond all recognition. The kidneys had also been removed from the body and placed on the table by the side of the breasts. The liver had likewise been removed and laid on the right thigh. The lower portion of the body and the uterus had been cut out and appeared to be missing. The thighs had been cut. The heart of the victim had also been removed but was never found.

A more horrible or sickening sight could not be imagined. The clothes of the woman were lying by the side of the bed, as though they had been taken off and laid down in an ordinary manner. While this examination was being made, the photographer who had been sent for arrived and took photographs of the body, the organs, the room, and its contents.

There was no appearance of a struggle having taken place, and, although a careful search of the room was made, no knife or instrument of any kind was found ...[v]

From the Journal of Jackson Kent

August 31, 1888

Victoria was in such a state tonight. I have tried to help her as best I can, but just when I think I am making headway, she regresses back into her addiction.

The most unusual thing happened to me on the way to Victoria. I ran into the most beguiling woman. She was tall, almost as tall as me. She had blonde hair that was tied back in a sultry bun, with wisps of hair surrounding her face. We literally bumped right into each other in the alleyway and every fiber of my being wanted to stay and talk with her, but I knew I had to go. Victoria needed me; she was the reason I was in Whitechapel at this ungodly hour of the morning. I didn't even get her name.

Speaking of the hour, I believe it is fair to assume that the beautiful creature I encountered was a prostitute.

I must find her.

September 1, 1888

I had hoped that my infatuation with the woman from last night would have abated by now, but I find that today I am more obsessed with finding her. I am not sure why she intrigues me so much, besides her obvious beauty ... there is something more. I have to know more about her.

I instructed Rothschild to find out what he could about the woman from last night. I didn't have a name and so I had him investigate all the public houses where prostitutes linger hoping to find work. He gave me a list of several and after dinner, I spent my evening in Whitechapel trying to find her.

After searching the first three from the list with no luck, I went into the Ten Bells Pub. I didn't have to see her, I knew the moment I walked in that she was there. What is this connection between us? I have never felt this pull before, not even with Charlotte.

Once I found her, I was reluctant to leave her. We had a few drinks and I brought her home. I knew the minute we began to speak that I had to find a way to see her again. So I came up with an agreement that I would pay her to stay with me indefinitely. As much as I hated paying her to be with me, I knew that if I didn't and she agreed to stay with me, she would lose her livelihood and I had to make sure that she would still earn some sort of income. To my great surprise, she agreed. Then again, why wouldn't she? I offered her a crown a night. Who does that?

She told me about a man that she lives with. She says that she doesn't love him, but stays with him out of gratitude. I can't help but be jealous of him.

This woman is going to break down all my walls. She will destroy me. I should just let her go.

September 2, 1888

I could not think straight today. Tonight is the first night of our agreement and I'm already a bundle of nerves. I can never let her see what she does to me. I must maintain control at all times.

We had a lovely dinner together, then we talked and I explained to her what I expect. There had to be some expectations, right? But at the same time I told her that nothing would happen between us that she didn't want to happen. Little did she know that I can make her want like she has never wanted before.

She is a strong, independent woman and her honesty is refreshing. However, she craves someone to take control of her mind and body. I intend on doing just that.

Kissing her is like dying and going to heaven. It was so hard for me to maintain control tonight. But I can't let down the walls, I can't let her see the closed-off beast inside. Not yet.

September 3, 1888

I realize today that I picked the perfect woman: sexy, beautiful, and discreet. She encountered her friends today in Whitechapel and kept our arrangement and everything about me to herself. I could not have been more pleased. So I rewarded her.

Who am I kidding, the reward was all mine. I pushed her beyond her limitations, I teased and tortured her in the most delicious of ways, and in the end I had to have her. Completely.

I knew she was going to be trouble. I knew she was going to test the walls that I have so strategically built. But I would not trade tonight for anything. I want more.

September 4, 1888

I am falling … Her beauty consumes me. I try to keep my distance, but my resistance is quickly fading.

September 5, 1888

I knew it. I knew she'd break through …

September 6, 1888

I can't get enough of her. She's intoxicating.

September 7, 1888

She has become my obsession. Her pleasure has become my mission. I'm lost in her and I can never let her know. She will consume me. She already consumes me. I need a distraction.

September 8, 1888

The old adage "Be careful what you wish for" was proven true today. I wanted a distraction and I got one: Victoria. My life's distraction. She has gone missing again and I have spent all day trying to find her, starting in the early hours of the day. Nothing. Where can she be?

September 9, 1888

Another day lost searching for my sister. Another day without Marie. I left without a note and without word as to where I was. If I was lucky, she would leave and I'd be rid of her. But I know deep down I can never be rid of her. In just a short time she has worked her way into my heart. I am falling in love with her.

I finally found Victoria, stoned out of her mind as I expected. I spent the remainder of the night nursing her back to some form of sanity. I wish she would just come home and let me care for her. Forget the opium and forgive me. She refuses, not that I ever get a lucid word out of her when we are together. But I will never break my vow to her. I will always be there for her, no matter what. Blood is blood.

September 10, 1888

I'm finally home and back with Marie. Victoria is settled for now.

I should have explained to Marie about my disappearance the minute I returned, but I did not. She was worried and concerned. I should have told her about Victoria before tonight. I should have trusted her. But I didn't.

Now she knows. I told her everything. And she gave me the greatest gift she could: her understanding.

September 11, 1888

I thought I would have tired of Marie by now. But that is not the case. She consumes me and I find instead of getting bored with her, I want more of her. Sex with Marie is mind-blowing. I love taking her to the brink only to leave her wanton and bereft. Teasing her and hearing her beg is my undoing. I can't get enough of her.

September 13, 1888

I am getting used to having Marie around. I wonder at times how I will live without her when she goes. And she will go. I don't know how or when, but I will lose her.

September 16, 1888

We have developed a routine like an old married couple. I find that I like it very much.

I ran into a rather odd gentleman today after leaving the House of Lords. I was walking toward the carriage and Carlton when out of nowhere a man appeared in my way and asked me for directions. When I give him what he asked, he politely asked that I write the directions down, as he would surely forget. I find that very odd; his destination was only two blocks away, due east. And really, do most people carry a writing instrument in their cloak? Odd, very odd indeed.

I brushed it off. Stranger things have happened.

September 22, 1888

The light in her eyes this evening was another gift. She got a new hat and I promised to take her to the theater. Why didn't I think to take her out before? I should be spoiling her like the queen that she is. I couldn't bear it if she left me now. She has destroyed all the barriers and walls that I have so carefully built and has worked her way into my heart. My heart has never felt so full, not even with Charlotte.

September 24, 1888

I bought Marie a dress to match her new hat. She still has not shown it to me, but Jasper described it in great detail. She is going to look like a vision tonight.

Tonight we attended the Union Jack at the Adelphi. We strolled the park while the Queen visited and dined at the Garden. The evening was magical and Marie shined like the lady that she is.

She truly was a vision. I had a special treat for her tonight in my bedchamber. I had planned to surprise her, but as always she surprised me first. She professed her love for me. At first I was angry, so angry that I wanted to punish her. When my grasp tightened around her throat, I truly believed that I would kill her. She panicked, but I could do nothing to stop the need to make her pay for her words. I couldn't release her.

As I watched the light leave her eyes, my orgasm struck me so strong and hard; the heightened sensations pulsed through my body. When I released her throat, I could tell by the look in her eyes that she was experiencing the same euphoria that I was. I expected her to run. I expected her to hate me. Instead, she gave me another surprise. She still loves me. And I rewarded her with my love in return.

I am finally free of the pains of my past.

September 25, 1888

Something has definitely shifted between us. We are in love and it's glorious.

September 27, 1888

I never believed I could love again. Losing Charlotte killed me inside; I was a shell of a man until now. I want to be her everything.

September 30, 1888

Victoria had another episode tonight. I reluctantly left Marie in our bed to tend to her. I love my sister, but this is getting tiresome. I wish there was more I could do, force her to leave this life. But everything I have tried fails.

Another murder in Whitechapel has occurred. Two women. I pray they catch this sadistic man.

October 1, 1888

My world is ending. The walls are closing in. Marie has left me. I have no idea why. Rothschild says she was upset and needed to leave in a hurry. Jasper says he left her in Whitechapel and that she asked him to tell me that she would return in a day or two. Why did she leave?

I will move heaven and earth to find her. I am lost without her.

October 2, 1888

Marie is still gone. I have not eaten in two days.

I've searched all the places that she frequented that I knew about. I've spoken to Madam Grace and even she has not heard from her. She needs to come home where she belongs. Why won't she come home?

October 3, 1888

Finally, my search for Marie has given me something to work with. Jasper has been questioning people in Whitechapel for two days now and has reported to me that a Mrs. McCarthy told him that she saw her at the Princess Anne Pub. It's the first lead we've had.

I leave for Whitechapel immediately.

Oh thank God, I've found her! She is drunk and dirty, but she is safe. She passed out not long after I arrived at her room. I've brought her home and had Eliza tend her. We will talk when she wakes and is feeling better.

October 4, 1888

I can't believe what she accused me of tonight. Well, she really didn't accuse me, but she implied ... she really thought that I am the murderer of Whitechapel. How absurd! How ridiculous! Have I given her any reason to think I could actually kill another human being? There are coincidences, I will give her that. But me, the man she says she loves, a murderer? I remained calm and I tried to convince her that I am not a killer. I made her look into my eyes and look at my hands. She could not deny that they were not the hands of a killer.

She's seen the error in her judgment. We are making our arrangement permanent; we are getting married.

October 5, 1888

I still find it hard to believe that she said yes and we are getting married. Victoria is missing.

October 6, 1888

I want to spend every waking minute with her. We've spent the afternoon amongst London's finest. Still no sign of Victoria. I worry for her safety.

October 7, 1888

The Dear Boss letter appears in the paper. Marie already knew his name and again, the coincidences between this sadistic man and myself are downright unnerving. Is he trying to set me up somehow?

Victoria is still missing. My men have searched the East End over and over. They have found nothing. What has happened to her?

October 10, 1888

We are making wedding plans. There is now a light at the end of my dark tunnel. I've found happiness again and this time, I will protect it with everything that I am. I will never take her for granted and we will grow old together.

Where is Victoria?

October 20, 1888

The wedding banns have been read. This is really happening. Marie is my soul and with her in my life, I am complete. I am no longer searching in the darkness for some form of happiness. I have truly found it.

Victoria has vanished. I am on pins and needles every day waiting to hear word that she has been found dead in an alley somewhere.

October 30, 1888

Marie wants a simple wedding. So do I. She also wanted me to take her back to Whitechapel today. At first I was skeptical, but I understand that she needs closure. Her life has changed drastically and she needs to say goodbye to her old ways and move on, feeling safe and content with me. So, we go to Whitechapel.

Our first stop, Miller's Court: Joe is an arse. How could she spend so much time with a man that treats her so rudely? His heart is breaking and I give him a little reprieve for that, but I still think he is an arse. I'm so glad that she no longer feels indebted to this man. Her loyalties lie with me now.

We also went to see two of Marie's friends, Julia and a Mrs. Harvey. Julia is quite the jealous individual but I guess all the women who work the streets in the East End dream of a prince coming to sweep them off their feet. It warms my heart to know that I am Marie's prince.

Julia and Mrs. Harvey had some information for us on Victoria and directed us to Madame Grace's establishment above the Ten Bells Pub. You can't imagine the shock of finding out that Victoria has been in the employ of Madame Grace, selling herself.

It was just my luck that she was there. We spoke. It didn't go well; our relationship is completely broken. I will still continue to care for her whether she wants me there or not, but she will never forgive my harsh words.

November 1, 1888

I have endured much heartbreak in my life, but having Marie in my life now has made up for it tenfold.

November 7, 1888

I love Marie's submission. Tonight, she was completely under my command.

November 8, 1888

She's gone! Jasper told me everything. How she compared my handwriting to the Ripper and how she was convinced that I brutally killed all those women. She never believed me. She believes that I am coming for her next. How could she? I should say good riddance, cut my losses, harden my heart and be done with such a woman who can't believe in me. But I can't do that. I'm a fool! I love her and I will find her.

Jasper and I spent all evening in Whitechapel. We went to her flat, the Ten Bells, the Britania, the Princess Anne, all the places that I knew she had frequented before. We went to Madame Grace's and spoke with her at great length. She was nowhere.

We questioned everyone that we passed on the streets. Some said they saw her drinking at the Ten Bells. Some said they saw her buy a candle at McCarthy's. And in the wee hours of the morning, many professed to seeing and hearing her. Apparently she was very drunk and singing down the streets. We checked everywhere. She was nowhere to be found.

November 9, 1888

Today's headlines leave me devastated. My heart has been obliterated and lies in fragments all over the floor. Marie has been found, but there won't be any chances of returning her home. The Ripper has gotten to her before I did. He destroyed her. He mutilated her. She is dead. My life is over and the walls around my heart turn to steel.

Inside the mind of a serial killer

They will never catch me ... I think as I sit here in this god-awful room waiting for her to return home. And I know she will. How do I know this? I know this because everything I've done up until this point has assured me that she will return here, on this night to face her fate.

Jackson Kent. I scoff. He was nothing but a puppet in my grand performance and soon he will be a victim. It was I that made sure they met in the alleyway the night I killed Mary Ann Nichols. It was I that made sure that Mr. Kent was away when Annie Chapman, Catherine Eddows, and Elizabeth Stride were murdered. You ask how? Well, I shall tell you.

Victoria Kent is a dear friend and a regular client of mine. She has been under my control for months. I manipulated her episodes so that they would occur at the same times as the murders of the first four women.

I also methodically planned each murder location so that they were closing in on Miller's Court. I wanted Marie to see that I was closing in on her. I believe I was quite obvious. I'll be surprised if she didn't see it coming.

I murdered her friend, Elizabeth Stride. Brilliant on my part. I deserve a pat on the back for that one.

But the best manipulation of all was the handwriting. One of my most clever and calculated moves; if I have to say so myself. One afternoon as Mr. Kent was leaving the House of Lords, I approached him and asked him for directions. And the clever part is that I asked him to write them down. Then, with a sample of his handwriting, I began to work on mastering his penmanship. Once I was satisfied with my forgery, I submitted a letter to The Boss, Central News Office. I knew, with her living in Kent's home, she would see his handwriting at some point once my letter was public information. And I knew that the police, Scotland Yard, and the press could not keep the letter quiet. I played them all perfectly.

I am so pleased with myself.

I pull the knife from my cloak. The silver shines in the candlelight and I revel in the feel of such an instrument. I run my finger ever so lightly along the knife's edge to feel its sharpness. *This will do nicely,* I think to myself. Placing it carefully back into my cloak, I wait.

I'm an actor on a stage. Each murder, a performance that outshines the last. Tonight will be my encore. The mutilations I have planned for Miss Kelly far exceed any of those performed on the other women. They were practice, stepping stones that I set up to prepare me for this last performance. She will know that this was all for her. She will know that these women died because of her. She will feel my pain and she will die.

Several minutes go by and then I see her small, frail hand reaching through the window to unlatch the door. She's here. My heart begins to race. The blood pulsing through my body in anticipation of what's about to happen causes my dick to grow hard and persistent with want.

She opens the door slowly and I can see the surprise and shock on her face. She knows who I am and she knows why I am here.

"What are you doing here?" she asks.

I rise from the chair and approach her. "I've come for you," I reply. I see no fear on her face, as if she was expecting this. Surely, she had to know. After everything that happened between us, she had to know that I would come for her and make her pay for the heartache.

"Are you ..." She stumbles over her words.

"You want to know if I'm the Ripper?" I reply, pulling the knife back out from my cloak. "What do you think, Marie?"

"And you have come for me?" she asks. I try not to laugh at her question. Is she serious? She continues, "I thought you ..."

I've had enough and I interrupt her. She is stalling and the absurdity of this line of questions angers me. Irritated, I say, "Surely you knew that you would be next."

"But it has been over a month since the last victim!" she cries out, as if that will save her. "Why murder more when you've gotten away with it?" I see confusion on her face and then she adds, "Why didn't you just come for me in the first place?"

I chuckle. "A serial killer never stops killing until he is caught. You've known that all along." I pause and then add, "Besides, stopping would ruin all the fun."

"Fun?" she questions. "You call these murders fun? Those poor women, how could you?"

"Oh Marie, you surprise me. You knew I wouldn't stop and you knew I'd be coming for you. Didn't you? Deep down in the depths of your soul, you've always known it was I. You questioned, you doubted, you even accused an innocent man unjustly. But deep down, you knew. That's why you kept coming back here. Subconsciously, you came to find me. Somehow you knew I would eventually be waiting right here for you." I see her shoulders slump and defeat is written all over her face. Ah yes, the submission gives me the greatest high. She is now mine.

"Now be a good girl and let me do what I came here to do. I need you to make this easy, Marie. Submit to me," I say calmly. I am surprised to see a twinge of defiance on her face.

"What if I don't?" she asks.

"Marie, you know better than to play power games with me. You know that all I have to do is command you and like the good little pet that you are, you will obey." I pause, waiting for a reaction. When there is none, I continue, "Lie on the bed, Marie." Without any hesitation, she does as she's told. Seeing her give up control makes me feel like a god. I can bend her to my will; I have all the control. And now my grand performance can begin.

"Anything you want to say before you can no longer talk?"

"I'm sorry for all the pain I caused you."

I'm sorry for you, Marie. You could have saved so many lives if you had said that a long time ago. It's a shame that you were selfish, headstrong, and didn't care about consequences. It's refreshing to see that you show some sign of remorse in the end. It's a pity that it's too late.

I take the knife and slash her throat.

Marie continues to bleed from her jugular as I continue to prepare the canvass of her murder. When I am done, I admire the work of art before me. It's my best work.

I leave the scene; her heart safely wrapped and tucked in my pocket. It's an odd thing to have in one's pockets, but I did say that her heart would be mine, and now, it is.

My work here is done. It's time for me to leave Whitechapel.

Look for a *Ripper* companion novella releasing in 2019 ...

INSIDE THE MIND OF A KILLER

Don't forget ...
If you've read Ripper and loved it, then please leave a review.
Authors love reading reviews!

ACKNOWLEDGEMENTS

As always, I would like to thank my friends and family. Without their support, I never would have the courage and the vision to become a writer.

My most heartfelt thanks goes to my husband Kevin. Another one of your ideas is being published and I am so glad that you encouraged me to write this. You are my muse babe, the voice in my head that is always encouraging me to broaden my writing abilities and to try new things. I love you for all that you are – thank you for this wonderful life.

I would also like to thank the members of my street team, Amy's Amazing Street Girls. You ladies are at the very top of my list and I am truly blessed to have you as a part of my team.

I would like to thank Alicia Freeman and Monica Diane. Your PR abilities are amazing. You are the best personal assistants a girl could have. You both are a pleasure to work with and I couldn't be more grateful for all you do for me. You ladies are superstars!

I'd like to thank Ellie and Carl Augsburger of Creative Digital Studios for their insightful ideas, creative marketing materials and comprehensive editing. I am beyond grateful to have such a talented team. You both are truly the best!

And finally, but definitely not least, I would like to thank Rebecca Weeks of Dark Wish Designs who has developed the perfect cover for Ripper. Your talents will never cease to amaze me.

ROMANCES WITH HEART

About the Author

Amy Cecil writes contemporary and historical romance. Her novel, Ripper is an erotic thriller, a new genre for her. When she isn't writing, she is spending time with her husband, friends and her four dogs.

She has held members in the Romance Writers of America (RWA) and the Published Authors Network (PAN). She was a winner in NanNoWriMo writing contests for the last three years and a nominee in the Metamorph Publishing's Indie Book 2016 contest in historical romance. She was also voted Favorite Historical Romance Author (2016-2017) in the Have you Heard Book Blog awards. Her Knights of Silence MC Series has won numerous awards, including Inks & Scratches Magazine's Best Couple in Love and Enchanted Anthologies Best Erotica of 2017.

She lives in North Carolina with her husband, Kevin, and their four dogs, Hobbes Koda, Karma and Katie.

Amy has several works in the works, including more to her Knights of Silence MC Series and her Pride and Prejudice Variations. She is also in three anthologies that will be coming out, Twisted Wonderland (August 2018), Love Eternal (October 2018) and Unmasking the Ripper (December 2018).

IN THE MEANTIME, SHE WANTS TO HEAR FROM YOU:

Amazon: https://www.amazon.com/Amy-Cecil
Goodreads: https://www.goodreads.com/authoramycecil
Webpage: http://acecil65.wixsite.com/amycecil
Facebook: www.facebook.com/authoramycecil

Amy's Street Team
Amy's Amazing Street Girls

Are you a member of Amy's street team? If not, you should be! We have all kinds of fun with free reads, sneak peeks, exclusives, games and a weekly SWAG BAG giveaway. Join us!!
https://www.facebook.com/groups/20903646918497/

Sign up for Amy's Newsletter and be in the know on all her latest news!
http://eepurl.com/cPYj3b

Want to talk more about Ripper? Join the spoiler group on FaceBook!!
https://www.facebook.com/groups/1764603363647008/

OTHER BOOKS BY AMY CECIL

HISTORICAL ROMANCE
A Royal Disposition:
myBook.to/ARoyalDisposition

Relentless Considerations:
myBook.to/RelentlessConsiderations

On Stranger Prides
myBook.to/OnStrangerPridesbyAmyCecil

Contemporary Romances

ICE:
getBook.at/ICEbyAmyCecil

ICE on FIRE:
getBook.at/ICEonFIREbyAmyCecil

Celtic Dragon:
getbook.at/celticdragonbyamycecil

Knights of Silence MC (Books 1 & 2):
mybook.to/KOSbyAmyCecil

Enemy Duet – Coming in 2019
Forgetting the Enemy
Loving the Enemy

Knights Series – Coming in 2019
Raw Honey
Sainte

REFERENCES

---

[i] *The London Gazette*, Newspaper, September 1, 1888

[ii] Dickens, C. (1850). The Personal History Of David Copperfield / by Charles Dickens; with illustrations by H.K. Browne. Bradbury & Evans.

[iii] Dickens, C. (1850). The Personal History Of David Copperfield / by Charles Dickens; with illustrations by H.K. Browne. Bradbury & Evans.

[iv] Dickens, C. (1850). The Personal History Of David Copperfield / by Charles Dickens; with illustrations by H.K. Browne. Bradbury & Evans.

[v] *The London Times*, November 9, 1888

Much of the Jack the Ripper historical information, press information, locations, timelines, etc. were found here:
Casebook: Jack the Ripper
http://www.casebook.org
Stephen P. Ryder & Johnno 1996-2018

Printed in Dunstable, United Kingdom